Have a Beautiful Day
Hot Air Balloons

—⚊—

a

Other Stories

To Bill + Marianne Goodheart

With love to you + yours,

L. J. Schneiderman

Jerry Schneiderman

ISBN-13: 9781495933912
ISBN-10: 1495933911
Library of Congress Control Number: 2014903190
CreateSpace Independent Publishing Platform
North Charleston, South Carolina

Acknowledgements

Most of these stories were previously published in the following literary quarterlies, Ascent, Black Warrior Review, Confrontation, Chouteau Review, Kansas Quarterly, Medical Heritage, Superstition Review, and as chapters in the books, *On Doctoring* (Simon & Schuster), *Grief and the Healing Arts* (Baywood Publishing), *Emergency Room* (Little Brown), and *Recognitions: Doctors & Their Stories* (Kent State University Press).

I also wish to acknowledge the copy editing help of Heidi Schneiderman, the early encouragement of the late Joanne Trautmann, and the wise editorial advice of Tom Parker and the late Audrey Curley.

Table of Contents

Sequel

It was right after Burt and Francine died that I began the saga of Joey Moxey the clown.

Tillie was too young for details, I thought, so I spared her—and myself. Burt had taken his wife to Warsaw where he had been invited to perform some of his music. Though she couldn't go, Tillie had been part of their excitement. When they brought her to stay with me she couldn't wait to trace her parents' journey on the map. She stumbled over her suitcases in her impatience, and there amid the clutter we both followed her small finger over the rumpled countries from the bed to the floor.

Never. Tillie grasped the concept right away. She repeated it to fix it in her mind. I saw the pain enter, briefly scorching her bright, solemn eyes. They closed deliberately and it was buried. She plucked at a band aid on her ankle. They'll never come back now.

Something went wrong with the plane and it fell down. She was seated on the edge of the table I had been sanding. Her face and limbs were scrawny, intense, her hair gritty, like coppery static. The smell of sawdust was still in the air. I pulled the plug out and wrapped the cord around the sander. I could not endure any more machinery noise that day.

Never.

It struck me that a child's world is made up of such categorical imperatives. Experiences are unique. Laws are absolute. You cannot have any candy. At Tillie's age it meant you can never have any candy. You must go to your room meant you must go there forever. My adult world by then had perverted nature, admitted relativity, forgiveness, recompense. I had grown soft.

In order to come to terms with what I had rediscovered—the uncompromising absurdity of the universe, I began to create the character of the clown. I told myself I owed it to my granddaughter, Tillie, to keep everything intact. Events were like pieces in a jigsaw puzzle, I said to her. By themselves they might look...well, weird. But they all fit together.

The truth is I had myself to persuade. Burt, my only son, was dead, and all the music the world would ever get from him ended. God knows it could have done with more.

At first the adventures of Joey Moxey were ordinary enough. He was your typical clown:

bald with a fringe of long hair around his head, red nose, baggy clothes, big feet. The feet were so big that in Joey's case one shoe also served as a sports car. Naturally he made his entrance by driving his shoe into the arena and when he stopped dozens of clowns tumbled out to the astonishment and delight of the children in the audience. They loved Joey Moxey and there was no better place in the world than under the enormous circus tent.

Joey had many adventures and he picked up a variety of friends in his travels, including a bird who made her nest on his head and flew out every time he took off his hat, Tina the cat, Oogak the jungle boy, and last but not least, Sadie Donut, a policewoman who followed him everywhere, presenting him with innumerable speeding tickets and parking tickets because she was so much in love with him. Their adventures would end in breathtaking escapes and Joey would hurry back to the circus tent just in time for the show to begin.

It was not long before my imagination ran out and it was up to Tillie to suggest subjects for the stories. Tell me about Joey Moxey falling off his bike, Tillie would say on a day she had had a catastrophic fall off her bike. And my story would being, "It just so happened Joey Moxey did fall off his bike..." And in the hundreds of nights that followed, it just so happened Joey

Moxey fell off a wall, spilled ketchup on his new clothes, got chased by a dog, bit by a cat, frightened by a snake, knocked over by a wave, awakened by a nightmare...

Tell me about Joey Moxey flying a plane, Tillie once said, and without hesitation, I launched into the fantastic adventure. "It just so happened, Joey Moxey did fly a plane once..." And I told how the clown and the President were the only two celebrities on board the maiden flight of a gigantic new supersonic plane when it developed engine trouble. The engine made such indescribable noises that the pilot fainted with fright. Joey Moxey took over. The control tower kept radioing instructions, but because this was such a new plane, no one knew exactly how it worked. Control tower would tell him to push a button on the elaborate instrument panel and when Joey pushed what he thought was the right button a wheel would fall off. Control tower would suggest something else, a lever perhaps, or a knob, or an overhead handle, and every time he followed the instruction another piece of the plane would disappear.

Things were getting precarious, and the complicated plane was getting smaller. But somehow the remarkable clown managed to bring it down with the quivering President on board who for his part managed to recover in time to make an inspiring speech to the gathered crowd of reporters and television cameramen. Joey Moxey was nowhere to be seen, of course, for he had slipped away to begin the show.

I was rather pleased with that story when I leaned down to kiss Tillie goodnight. Her eyes were somber, her face wet with tears. "You're never serious," she whispered angrily, and I lay there beside her, wondering at my need to deceive her, until she fell asleep.

Burt had inherited my stark baldness. I had shaved my head until the sixties when I adopted his long-haired style for the fringe around my skull. We were an amusing pair then, and friends were always telling us how much we looked alike. But it wasn't until that night I realized how much we had in common with the remarkable clown.

When Burt and Francine were killed I worried briefly that Francine's folks would seek custody of Tillie. Not that I would have contested it. I loved Tillie, wanted only the best for her, and could recognize the arguments on their behalf. The Oaks were a married pair as solid as their name; whereas I lived alone, Sarah and I having parted long ago. Duncan Oaks had already "put money away" for retirement while I have never really considered retirement, it always having been my natural life-style.

But I underestimated Duncan's and Mattie's determination to follow their own rainbow to its end—a condo in Florida, surrounded by water and golf courses, with assured re-sale potential. "This is no environment to bring up a little girl," Duncan crooned petulantly. I agreed. Besides, he complained, they had worked hard all their lives, held off, sacrificed, deprived themselves. They owed themselves this. They deserved it. In agitated voices made scratchy by the long-distance wires they told me of the tickets they had bought for tours, boat trips, chartered planes, vacation clubs. I agreed with their good judgment. Tillie should stay with me.

Tillie stayed with me. She followed me everywhere. For a while I worried about her attachment to me. Every time we were near each other she had to hug me, every time we passed we had to kiss. Tillie's kiss was a darting wetness, a sparrow sound. Was I somehow the living ghost of her father, the death and rebirth? *But I was never serious.* Was I the embodiment of the spirit of Joey Moxey, the clown? The questions formed in Tillie's eyes, glowed like hot sand. *And the answer?* Perhaps it was there for a moment, a brief shadowy scowl. Then gone. Her eyes again caught streaks of sunlight, as did her hair, which scattered about her in curls as though charged with electricity.

"Joey Moxey can be more than a clown," Tillie reproached me. "Joey Moxey is happy being a clown," I insisted. Her voice cracked.

Tillie talked so often with an adult's sense of the world that I was taken by surprise whenever she broke down and wept over simple childish things.

I knew it was not considered healthy for Tillie to come home after school and stay with me rather than find friends to play with. These were dangerous signs of social maladjustment. But for Tillie, these maladjusted moments seemed her happiest ones. She had inherited not so much my love of solitude as my penchant for intimate experience.

Not surprisingly she was exquisitely musical. She asked to learn the cello, Burt's instrument, and I managed to find a small size second-hand one and fix it up for her. I could never understand music. In Burt's case it was like an underground spring that broke open some time in his childhood and never stopped bubbling. He was a furious worker. Even before his teens Burt was practicing long hours in his room. When it was silent it meant he was composing. There was nothing we needed to do to encourage such onrushing talent, but keep out of the way. When Burt grew older, his music seemed to grow firmer, more self-assured. Like his voice. And like his voice it deepened, became gentle, more resonant.

Where all this came from I'll never know. Sarah's only distinct talent and obsession was for alcohol, and I was lazy, frankly and peacefully so. I once played the piano, but let it drift when my parents decided lessons were too expensive. I'm a good, but rather slow moving sort of furniture maker.

Tillie, though she could hardly have known Burt as a man, having barely known him as a father, seemed destined to follow his career. When she came home from school she joined me with her cello, whether outside in the backyard under the fruit trees, in the workshop or in the kitchen. She even played as I sat on the toilet.

The night of the day Tillie fell and gashed her wrist which required stitches and prevented her from practicing her cello I told her it just so happened Joey Moxey had cut his hand before a concert, but he carried it off anyway by hiding Tina the cat inside his cello and having her sing Bach's Sarabande for the Unaccompanied Cello, which happened to be Tillie's favorite piece at the time. The audience loved it. Joey made it to the circus on time. And Tillie, bandaged arm on the pillow, fell asleep.

Naturally, it was not possible for Tillie to avoid alienating her schoolmates. They did not like this lonely creature who found so many levels of meaning in child's play. They were suspicious of her laughter, which expressed a pleasure in too many things at once. And yet, serious as she was, she did not take the important things seriously enough. This was my fault.

I had trouble keeping up with the laundry, much less with the styles, and instead of brightly colored variations on fashion jeans, Tillie more often than not wore plain, faded dresses.

And her knowledge of boy's anatomy disconcerted them. I told her that it was a matter of principle never to strike in the vulnerable area unless the boy fought unfairly. To her credit Tillie reserved this weapon for just such occasions. Once however, she temporarily disabled a teacher, and I had to pay a visit to Principal Rodney's office.

Tillie was exercising her right of free expression, I said. (She had remained seated for the Pledge of Allegiance the day after the President was pictured smiling with another Latin American dictator). The teacher who hauled her up by the hair was committing assault and battery. Principal Rodney assured me things were quite the other way as measured by the outcome.

They gave her more room from then on, but did not stop laughing at her, teachers as well as children. It just so happened that everyone laughed at Joey Moxey too when he was little, I said. Which is why he decided to become a clown. Instead of feeling sorry for himself, he came to love his unique gift. Unhappy people fear their uniqueness; happy people love their uniqueness. This too, I think, Tillie understood.

She was standing on the bathtub swinging her brown lunch bag while I was sitting on the toilet. How many times now I found myself issuing proclamations from that throne. My bowels, which all my life scarcely had been more noticeable than my breathing or my heartbeat, had become rebellious of late. I had reached the Metamucil age.

Fortified with the lessons of Joey Moxey, Tillie went off to school. The lessons barely held to the end of the school day when Tillie would come racing home, her eyes moist, her cheeks drained, more often than not to greet me where she had left me, on the toilet. This was good for a bedtime story, of course. It just so happened that Joey Moxey was sitting on the throne when the King and Queen of England decided to pay him a surprise royal visit with all their lords and ladies.

Tillie and I talked quite thoroughly about things, probably more than the things deserved. But we enjoyed talking. She would set up her cello as I warmed the chocolate milk. Out of this would come a discussion of motion. The vibration of the cello string, the melodic movement of sound, the stirring of the molecules of chocolate milk as it became warm. We imagined ourselves as molecules of chocolate milk, part of a delicious storm of other chocolate molecules. Would we recognize each other as we flew by? Would we see each other again? Would we remember each other as we grew old?

She helped me with my work. I showed her how to drive 20d nails into three-inch planks. It took sensitive hammering. The wood was hard and full of knots—one had to *find* the hole—and a clumsy swat would curl the nail.

Or sometimes she would sit beside me as I worked on my plastic bottle sculpture. There was a time when I had first begun that I would take plastic bottles and with great enthusiasm cut them and twist them and melt them into all sorts of peculiar shapes. It was my rococo period. As I grew older I began to adopt a more classical approach. Michelangelo once said he tried to *free* the sculpture from the block of stone. And so did I with plastic bottles. Each bottle I discovered had all the elements of its sculpture within it.

Tillie would stop playing and watch quietly as I held a bottle in my hand, turning it over and examining it. Suddenly, almost as though a dressmaker had drawn a pattern, the pieces would declare themselves. With a linoleum cutter I would slice the bottle along the lines and assemble them. Tillie was always delighted. You see, I said, what people saw as the purpose of the bottle—what they bought it for in a store—that was really not its purpose, but only its transitional state. Its real purpose was to stand there along with all the other plastic bottle spirits scattered through our house and back yard.

"Why don't you sell them?" Tillie asked.

"Because no one would buy them," I answered.

"Why wouldn't anyone buy them?"

"Because I wouldn't sell them."

"Why wouldn't you sell them?"

"Because no one would buy them."

Tillie slapped her cello furiously. "Must you always talk like a clown?"

But she laughed when I nodded yes.

Tillie was always clinging to me, yet she was never possessive. When she came home from school she would find a customer in my workshop now and then, a fashionably dressed woman on a spree or a decorator looking for some odd piece among my sprawling chairs and strange tables. Tillie would listen with delight to the conversation. I would catch her eyes glowing on me. She knew I was charming our guest. If I really liked the woman I would pour her some beer in a hollow-stem champagne glass and hold it up high as I passed it to her, the bubbles glittering in the sunlight. The women were invariably delighted. I made them feel comfortable. I was easily pleased.

And if Tillie saw them at breakfast the next morning she greeted them cheerfully and hugged them too before going off to school.

Once she wandered into the bedroom while my houseguest was still in bed. I was shaving.

Fascinated, Tillie climbed up on the sink and followed my stroking closely. The houseguest looked up somewhat disconcertedly, a condition that was not alleviated very much by the conversation that followed.

"When I grow up, do you think I should shave," Tillie asked, "or should I let my beard grow?"

"It all depends, Tillie," I answered without hesitation. "Whatever you think looks best on you."

We laughed and wrestled on the bed, and Joey Moxey decided to let his beard grow until it was so long he tripped on it as he ran and when he tried to untangle himself it got caught between his toes and in the carburetor of his shoe. Eventually it so locked him up into a ball of fuzz that Sadie Donut had to roll him, dust, dirt, sticky wads of chewing gum and all, into a trough of hair remover. Which is why Joey Moxey had no hair except for the fringe around his head. But this only made Sadie Donut love him more, for to her he seemed handsomer than ever.

But that night, Tillie came home from school, her eyes burning with rage. "It's not true. Girls don't grow beards!"

I nodded solemnly.

"You're never *serious.*" Tillie protested. "How do you expect to *amount* to anything?"

As she ran off to fetch her cello, I wondered what moment in Tillie's school had first shined light on the phrase "amount to anything."

The next day I spurted blood into the toilet bowel.

Dr. Chernock had a polished brass nameplate, British magazines in the waiting room and a long snaky instrument with which he peered inside me. I heard him groan impatiently—"Oh, Ah..." as he struggled with some invisible and apparently unappreciative part of my body. Then suddenly he issued a triumphant sigh. "Eureka, I found it." He snapped off his rubber gloves and reassembled his French cuffs. It was cancer, he said.

That night, it just so happened Joey Moxey was subjected to the same curious procedure. A very famous scientific institute was interested in doing research on the famous clown to find out what made him so funny. They kept him in the research institute subjecting him to all sorts of elaborate chemical analyses while Nobel-prize winning scientists paraded back and forth between his bed and mahogany paneled conference rooms. Until at last, one of the scientists, while peering in the most unlikely place through a long snaky tube, cried, "Eureka! I found it!"

When it came time to kiss her goodnight, Tillie kept her head buried under the pillow.

The next day, Dr. Chernock admitted me to the hospital. He assured me he looked forward to ridding me of this annoyance. Tillie stayed with a neighbor.

The night before surgery Tillie took her bedtime story in my bed for a change. It just so happened Joey Moxey was in the hospital with a runny nose. It was a bad runny nose, of course, and soon the great clown ran out of Kleenex. He called for the nurse, but she was too busy to come, so Joey had to shift for himself. Out of bed he stumbled and into the next room where he helped himself to a handful of Kleenex. The patient in the room awoke from a deep sleep just in time to see the weirdest sight he had ever seen: a clown blowing his nose with all his might. Poor Joey. He had to blow so hard that his red ball of a nose collapsed and only gradually swelled up again with a long eerie whistle.

You can imagine what this did to the patient's nerves. He lay there absolutely transfixed until this apparition's nose finally stopped growing and the long eerie whistle came to an end.

No sooner was Joey Moxey gone than the terrified patient rang for the nurse. And no sooner did the nurse hear the patient's ridiculous story than she decided he must have been awakened by a nightmare and presented him with an enormous sleeping pill. Zonk went the patient. Out cold. Meanwhile, in and out of all the rooms went Joey in his never-ending lust for more Kleenex. And from every room came the same frightened ringing for the nurse. The nurse could not understand why all her patients were suddenly having such wild night-mares, but she had no doubt how to deal with the problem. Every one of the patients got the same treatment. And every one of them went Zonk. Out cold.

The next morning when the doctor arrived he found all his patients absolutely stretched out, snoring, unarousable. Except for poor Joey Moxey who was sitting up in bed, still blowing his nose. When the nurse saw him she began to think she was having her own nightmare.

Tillie tried, but she couldn't help it—soon she was laughing uncontrollably, particularly at the sound effects, and when I kissed her goodnight from the bed I felt the tears—this time of happiness; though they flashed with the memory of sorrow.

The surgery was over quickly.

I had heard stories about patients being strangely aware during an operation despite the anesthesia. But for these stories I would assume I had been visited by my own bad dreams. I remembered visions, starkly colored and vibrating with sound, which must have taken place during the depths of my uncon-sciousness or during my fitful awakening in the recovery room. I remember faces appear-ing suddenly, hands groping toward my wrist, other hands moving like mountains, burying me in their darkness. Somewhere within all this unreal universe I heard something very real, the great hollow groan of disappointment as Dr. Chernock looked inside and saw that it was too late.

When the surgeon appeared again at my bedside his mood was much changed. He seemed resentful. Gone were optimism and gracious enthusiasm, the powers he had brought to bear on his patients' behalf. These, and the magic of his scalpel were what he had counted on to drive away the evil cancers. I had let him down, demeaned him. His mood told me all, though in specific words Dr. Chernock told me nothing.

That night Joey Moxey was visited in the hospital by all his friends and they put on a show for the patients. My voice faded and Tillie finished the story for me. She said everyone in the hospital loved the performance except for one person. Guess who. The nurse. She was bored by it all and fell fast asleep. It hurt so much when I laughed that I begged Tillie to stop. She kissed me goodnight and left.

The next day Dr. Chernock told me I could leave soon and recuperate at home. He suggested that I find another doctor. He was a specialist, a surgeon, and his services would no longer be necessary.

That night it just so happened Joey Moxey's runny nose got worse and worse and to everyone's disappointment he died.

For an instant Tillie's eyes flared at me.

All of Joey's friends gathered to see what should be done. Sadie Donut led the discussion. They wondered whether they should bury him or cremate him. After hardly any debate they agreed that the clown would have wanted them to find out whichever was cheaper and be done with it. They reminisced, of course, about all the wonderful adventures they had had with him. No doubt about it, there would never be another Joey Moxey. But Sadie Donut pointed out that Joey would have been the first to say that about them, too. She for one would continue to have adventures even without Joey Moxey, and she was sure everyone else would do the same. But, she said, wouldn't Joey Moxey want them most of all to continue being friends, meeting, and sharing with each other all the things that happened?

That night as Tillie and I kissed, the tears that flashed between us were hers and mine.

The next night, Tillie climbed up on my bed and began the saga of Sadie Donut.

Comfort Care

Father Julian Chiochio's Comfort Care Group. *An oasis of old-fashioned humanity in the high-tech desert of the modern hospital,* the article called it. And a picture showed Father Julian protruding his jaw in what could have been compassionate exhortation or the effort to dislodge something stuck in his teeth. It struck her as a lot better way to mark time while waiting to make babies than subbing for burnt-out teachers in South-Central L.A. Whatever makes you happy, her husband Jonathan said.

The operator paged Father Julian and put him through; she heard his gravelly voice on the other end of the line: Sure, what the hell, join the crowd, the more the merrier. Followed by a weird almost barking kind of laugh.

The next morning while they passed around sticky buns and coffee he asked: What's your name? Kiki, she told him. Kiki Fishberg. No kidding. Again that strange laugh, a cough mostly. Call me Woppy. We'll be the Seven Dwarfs. To her dazzlement the others picked up on it right away; they started working on Dwarf names. Sarah, one of the nurses became Lumpy. Maynard the psychologist became Bitchy. Deenie, another nurse, Mammoplasty. Ruth, the social worker, Emesis. Sam, the psych resident, Fuckup. Embarrassed, she felt her face erupt in a tingling heat, but by the time they had gone around she had tucked her stocking feet under her, joined the laughter, and was bouncing up and down in her chair. You see, he said. The way we rev ourselves up.

He mocked everything you would expect of priests. Instead of a clerical collar he wore rumpled shirts and loose clashing ties picked up years ago at Goodwill outlets, when you still could get bargains, he said. And pushed behind his ears what was left of his gray hair, securing it with thick black-rimmed glasses and a scrutty ponytail. Sloping nose, tangled brows, moist lips, a tongue always in motion, shaping some raunchy joke, usually, as though it were his idea of a fine cigar. Not at all attractive. And not exactly mainstream thanatology. He made a feast of foul words as though they were one of the last great pleasures of life. People don't give a fuck about heaven or hell. They just want to die in their sleep.

But everything the article said was true—he brought people comfort. At the bedside he would deposit his thick hand, this huge clod wormy with veins, unerringly on the part of the body that hurt the most. And it never failed—eyes squinting like a cowboy's against hot gritty wind would instantly soften and a gaunt face would fill up and smile.

Her first solo assignment was a Mrs. Bogatescu with breast cancer. One after another silent explosions of masses in her armpits, under her ribcage, circling her neck had exhausted her husband and two children to the point that they could no longer bear to be with her; nor was she in her denuded almost embryonic shapelessness able to summon up the stoicism necessary to keep them brave. The woman spent most of her waking hours weeping.

Which is what Kiki found herself doing at morning report. She shook her head with embarrassment. For Chrissake! She had been on the case less than a week! But Father Julian looked at her. I'll come with you today.

As usual they just sat there at first, the only sound the muted racket from the hallway outside. Then with one hand in Mrs. Bogatescu's, the other settled on a mound of flesh, Father Julian began his routine. He was curious. How had she met her husband—what was his name? Chuck. How had she met Chuck, tell me about it—Where? When?—waiting patiently in the long silences. The woman's lips nibbled against gluey saliva. Funny story. They met. At this gas station. Chevron—they took Mastercard. While trying to figure out how to use the pump. This guy came over. Soon Father Julian and Mrs. Bogatescu—Carla—were laughing over the crap game called love. What if their gas tanks hadn't been in synch? What if Chuck had come a few minutes earlier, or she a few minutes later? They had achieved simultaneous gasups, so to speak. What if, what if—the possibilities and *double entendres* were limitless. By early afternoon they were reveling in the unforgettable adventures of Carla and Chuck. And Mona and Thelma—by the time night came around she was gasping out her daughters' favorite scatological jokes, a faint blush on her yellowish face, joining Father Julian with her croaky laughter until exhausted she fell into a deep sleep and died.

Kiki found herself being awakened by Father Julian gently stroking her hair. Outside the black windows traffic slid by, clicking like tumblers behind a safe. Want some coffee, he said. She looked at her watch. Jonathan would already have taken his dinner into the bedroom to pore over loose-leaf binders. He was in the management training program of a large detergent company. She had learned to fall asleep in the glow of his desk lamp. Coffee sounded nice, she said.

They drove in his unconvertible convertible, an old Karmann Ghia whose shredded top wouldn't go up—in the dash lights it looked like something made of dried mushrooms. What about when it rains, she asked. He jutted his thumb toward the back: a poncho.

They shared a peach tart, picked at it listlessly in one of the leatherette booths, their eyes half-closed and swollen. She found herself showing him pictures from her wallet. What is this she wondered, his routine again? But he looked at each one methodically, tilting it under the fluorescent lights. Mother, father, sister, Jonathan. He liked Jonathan. Good looking. No, better than that. Corporate looking, know what I mean? Graduation portrait, wedding shots. It annoyed her now, that same chipmunk smile stamped on her face. Her childhood, she thought for the first time. What's this, he said. It was a honeymoon shot, both of them crouched in parkas, her left hand bulbously swathed in bandages—this huge Q-tip. Jonathan's idea, to camp across the country. Naturally, the first night out while trying to cook dinner in the dark she practically cut her thumb off. Almost in reflex Father Julian's hand plopped down and covered hers. Then quickly he smiled, patted it ironically. They both laughed. The routine. Anyway, no problem. She has a Cuisinart now and a clean well-lighted kitchen. What about you, she said. Any pictures? No, sorry. No pictures, no family. He'd grown up in foster homes, mostly. Could he go for another peach tart? Why not, he said.

So, she said when he came back with the tart. That it? Deprived childhood? The coffee, she realized, was beginning to kick in. That how come you're so weird? She flicked her fork toward his purplish plaid shirt and yellow and black tie.

He shrugged. Not all that weird. You end up wearing what you wore in college. Back then everyone dressed like this. The only rebellious thing he did those crazy days was become a priest. It appealed for some reason. Discipline.

She said it sounded like something out of a porno mag.

He gave his barking laugh and looked at her, startled obviously, but not without admiration. Well, I suppose. Celibacy. Just another form of pornography.

The weirdest of them all too seems to me.

He rubbed his face. It helps me keep the faith. He rubbed again. You keep the faith hoping someday to believe. What about you?

She told him God was not one of her hangups. Far as she was concerned, far as what she believed—and she thanked her Cognitive Science major for this—religion was wired into the brain just like hunger, thirst, lust, what have you. Survival of the species, that's all. Otherwise homo sapiens would've looked around eons ago at all the shit going down and said, What's the use, Why go on? You remember the Stockholm Syndrome? These women held hostage by a gunman who threatened to kill them. What'd they do? They fell in *love* with the bastard. They began to *worship* him. Even though he didn't give a *shit* about them. That's religion, far as I'm concerned—a humongous Stockholm Syndrome. She was Jewish, of course, if anyone asked. But all that meant is she was brought up to celebrate Hanukah along with Christmas (lighting a Menorah and topping the tree with the Star of David) and knew the way to make her parents happy was by marrying Some Nice Jewish Boy Like The Jonathan Feldman Boy.

Through the whole thing Father Julian sat hunched over his coffee, amused not so much by what she said, she knew, but by the way she said it, his brow furrowed with that kind of ironic skepticism you see in French movies. She liked that. When she was in the mood to be cynical—and coffee unfailingly stirred it up—she would perch up on her stocking feet and flop her hair about, very much aware that her *petite*-ness took on a particular archness that men found stimulating. In fact the only thing lacking to make this cafe scene French-perfect, she thought, was the sensual wreathing of cigarette smoke. But she didn't smoke and was just as glad Father J didn't either.

In the room, while you were sleeping, he said. I was watching you.

She blinked. Oh yeah?

The way you were sitting. The way you were...draped. Bathsheba. By Rembrandt. You know that one? She shook her head. She must have died while I was looking at you. And I thought: It's true. Life *is* short. Art *is* long. He laughed and ended up coughing and punching his chest comically. They agreed—time to be getting home.

The next time she needed help it was Mrs. Kettleman, an old black woman with white hair and bowel cancer. In an effort to stifle her pain the medical resident had given her larger and larger doses of intravenous morphine and ended up shutting down her bowels. For the last two days the old woman had been vomiting so wretchedly the doctor avoided her room. This time they not only sat with her, but Father Julian showed her how to give a bed bath. Twice—when they didn't get the kidney basin up in time—they rolled her from side to side and changed the rank swampy sheets. As Father Julian ran the washcloth over the prunish body, lifting the flaps of her breasts to clean under them, Kiki felt a wave of heat flood her face. For Chrissake—what was going on? She shook her head, felt her hair sting her ears.

This time the coffee only made her more agitated. Her ankles banged against each other on the chair.

What I want to know is what would've happened if we weren't there?

Well for one thing it would've been a lot worse, wouldn't it.

That's what I mean, that's just what I *mean*. I mean does it *have* to be so fucking ugly?

Why we were there, right? So it wouldn't be.

Oh, nice. Some people get to throw up so that other people can feel good about wiping it off.

What can I say? The ways of the Lord are mysterious.

She felt her hand tighten around her coffee cup, actually saw it turn white, saw it bulge at the base of her thumb, like an adder puffing.

You, he said quickly—he launched a mocking finger, which made an aborted bulky dive like something shot from a circus cannon—*you* got the answers, not me. And in the midst of his protracted laughing and coughing she jumped up, knocking the table, spilling the coffee.

Then the fantasies began. At first they were the kind of harmless pleasures some of her old college professors had inspired: soaring in a balloon, rolling in waves, seatmates on a hijacked jet, sweaty rock singers joined over a spotlit mike, that sort of thing. She let herself enjoy them, why not. Time and again the Anne Tyler book she was reading in bed would drop on her chest. Startled, she realized she was imagining his thick hands washing *her* body, lifting *her* breasts. It terrified her—this idea, this *image* of her emaciated body; she actually sneaked her hand under the sheet and rolled her plump breasts for reassurance; and lay awake waiting for Jonathan to come to bed. But when he moved in and entangled her legs she couldn't help imagining that it was Father Julian. Still that was okay. Nice, actually. Only when Father J's massive face began to haunt her dreams, when things started getting out hand, did she get uneasy.

It was amazing in retrospect that no one in the group said anything about that barking laugh, his cough—which kept getting worse and worse—until a patient on rounds pointed out what was obvious: You really ought to go see a doctor about that. The group all laughed, but really it was true. They had just gone along with it as one of their beloved leader's peculiarities.

Sure enough, the chest X-ray showed trouble. And one of his testicles was more like a rock, which on biopsy proved to be cancer. The group was stunned. You of all people, they said. Why not me of all people? And he cursed abundantly to keep the group's spirits up. If I had been using the fucking things—fucking things, right?—if I'd been using them I would have been checking on them. Gathered around his bed they laughed, albeit with some constraint. Soon everyone in the hospital was repeating his latest quip. They could just as

well lopped off my appendix for all the difference it makes.

Now her fantasies took on a vividness, a
microscopic glow and particularity she found
breathtaking. As though she and the cancer—
like terrorists from opposite sides—had met
and formed a conspiracy of expediency. They
would seep into his flesh, divide the territory,
occupy, possess. Borders and rules were for others, not for them. Picture this: what if, what *if*
one night while he was lying there she entered
his room and before he said a word climbed on
top of him, engulfed him, pressed him down,
invading his mouth with her tongue, digging
into his anus with her finger the way she did
in the heat of making love. What would he do,
what would he *do*? The scene's sheer implausi-
bility made her feel free to let it loose, let it fly
unchecked. His mouth, her tongue; his anus,
her finger. It became an obsession—it would
never happen—what harm then? Except that
now when Jonathan turned off the light and
came to bed she pulled him onto her, and even
though with the utmost sweetness he complied
with all her requests she was left sleepless and
thrashing.

Tenacious spots remained on the X-ray.
Specialists conferred. Another biopsy.
Chemotherapy had failed. Law and order had
given way. Like a fanatic mob cells were riot-
ing through the alleys of the lung. The fiery

drugs left him wide-eyed and ashen, like someone pulled from a car wreck. He would feel better in a few days, they said. But now when the group assembled around his bed there was an audible heave of dismay. Fucking Jesuitical cancer, Father Julian whispered. What did you expect? But the laughter churned and died.

She figured out ways to be alone with him—after the others in the group had gone home, after visiting hours, between nursing shifts, best of all in the evening right after medications. She too would ignore restraints. She had bonded with her enemy the way generals do who keep a picture of their adversary before them. At first she sat, just as she had been taught, held his hand as he fell asleep, nothing more. But one night she lay her head down and felt—a gasp escaped her—his other hand come down. She seized it, pressed down on it with all her might, felt it deep in her hair, holding, holding fast.

At last he was deemed strong enough to go home. It was Kiki's suggestion that the group look in on him now and then to help him with his laundry, the cleaning, garbage, shopping and such. All agreed—she had the most free time.

That morning she pranced back and forth in front of the mirror and flung what must have been a dozen outfits on the bed. What does a priest's housekeeper *wear*? The spearmint dress looked too minty, the denim wraparound too suggestive, shorts—now that the weather had turned chilly—too blatant. Tweeds? Jeans? Forget leather. Flinging, flinging. Her one cashmere sweater was flattering but too Symphony Boardish, her baggy turtleneck too artsy fartsy, worse it made her boobs look like day-old bread. For Chris*sake*! She blindly stabbed into her closet and hauled out white cotton pants. Okay. Next. What she always wore around the house with them: a T-shirt. She threw it on. Done. Finished. Decided. She slammed the door and hurled herself down the steps as though leaving the scene of a crime.

He lived toward the back of a pinkish two-story singles complex which featured stenciled parking spaces and an oval swimming pool. The crucifix was there, just as she expected, stark and assertive as she opened the door. Yet it was as though he had made this one brutal sweep of his arm across the wall to clear it then could do no more. The rest was a dizzying mess, as though the whole place had been tipped on its side. Newspapers, magazines, books, shoes, towels, cereal boxes, Kleenex, tuna fish cans, abandoned dishes—she had to pick her way. Wrinkled Venetian blinds scattered pale pink light into a dank smell of immobility. The man himself was off in a corner, gloomily watching acrobatic ski jumpers on television. Gray sweatshirt and milky blue pajama bottoms. His terry cloth bathrobe lay open revealing puckered folds of flesh.

Then for the first time it occurred to her: This will not be easy. And stood there wondering how to begin.

I've come to cheer you up, she said. Cheerily. Don't make my trip a total waste of time.

He grimaced, lurched a bit—a laugh? A cough? I know the routine, he said. All the tricks.

She sighed. Her shoulders fell. I know you know. She started going around, picking things up, pushing other things into more or less piles.

Look at that, he said. Ski jumpers used to be happy if they could just come down on their skis. Now they do all these fucking loops. The bursts of cheers from the TV caused him to cringe.

Like bagels and croissants, she said. You don't get the plain old-fashioned kind any more. She started slapping books into the bookcase. *Greek Bronze Statuary, Russian Art Nouveau, Paintings of the Lotus Sutra.* She saw he had an Escher print on the wall. In college she had studied Escher four different times—in Art History and again in Cognitive Psychology and again in Modern Philosophical Theories and again in a course entitled Man and Machine: Is There a Difference?

Must you make all that noise?

That's why I'm here. To ruin your day.

He still didn't take his eyes off the TV. He was armed, prepared. He would not be provoked. He would not be comforted. She started stacking the dishes. On the way to the kitchen she was brought to a halt by his surly voice.

Lucky you, they said. Cancer of the testicle we can cure. Completely. Permanently. Ninety percent of the time.

She turned and looked at him.

I'm one of the ten percent. Don't look at me like that. I'll throw you out. He lurched again, a low-pitched rumble, it hardly made a sound. One of the Chosen People. Like you.

She put down the dishes and came back to him, was about to take his hand, but caught herself. Careful. One of the tricks. Instead she kneeled down next to him, pushed her face between him and the TV. Look at me when you talk, she said.

You want to know how I feel?

She nodded.

Like the punchline in a bad joke.

That's better, she said. He scowled. Not a trick, she said hastily. Sarcasm. Honest. It just slipped out. When was the last time you ate?

He lifted his elbow in the direction of a bowl yellowed with grit. She picked it up. I'm not hungry, he said. Remember, I know them all. His hand toyed with a plastic container of pills. Then dropped it on the table next to

him. Then picked it up again. She took the
container out of his hand. Morphine for pain.
Come on, she said. You need a shower. She
heaved him up by the lapels of his robe. He
looked at her startled. Come on. Which way?
Glowering. This he was not prepared for. She
gave him a push and started working off his
bathrobe, pushing, raising his arms and haul-
ing his sweatshirt over his head, getting a pun-
gent whiff of each item as she flung it behind
her.

The hallway was crowded on both sides with
scrambled books and boxes filled with record
albums—mostly operas, it seemed. On the walls
were a few unframed oil paintings, sheepishly
crude and scratchy. Yours? she asked as they
came to the first one. He grunted. A murky
cafe scene showing old men playing odd instruments including one with a broom handle
sticking out of a can. He waved his hand giving
his undershirt a flip as they went by. Florence.
The next, an old woman and man scraping the
hull of a boat—mostly muddy blue and green.
Bellagio. She reached around and started
working on the knotted drawstring. Then the
largest picture of all, full of agitated colors, a
young woman slouched by a stone fountain.
Another wave of the hand. Bathsheba. Me, you
mean? They paused to look at it. The face was
so crudely done it could have been anyone.
You, he said. And me. Aha, she said. He turned

and looked at her and started to sway and for a moment she thought she was going to have to grab him, but he caught himself on the wall and turned and she got back to work, bumping him forward with her body. The last thing she pulled off was his pajama bottoms, stepping on them to keep them anchored while he shuffled out of them. By the time they reached the bathroom he was naked.

To keep from embarrassing him she occupied herself with the shower. Let's see. How do these things work? It's been so long.

The stall was one of those single-piece units made of a white plastic, the door was frosted sliding glass, the showerhead the kind popular in motels that could be adjusted to give pulsating jets of water. Only after she got it going did she turn and let herself look at him. She had to, of course. Really look at him.

It was what she had always heard—the eyes of an animal before slaughter. Not for food though, nothing so rewarding as that, but because he was no longer any use. His torso slack, his arms, which he held in front of him, thin with furry burs of hair. And his buttocks— truly negligible. Negligible, that's all she could say. She was used to Jonathan's bulk.

Come on, she said. In you go. But he didn't move. And she realized it would never work, unless...unless...And with a sweep of her hand threw back her hair. And took off her clothes.

For a while they just stood there, the two of them, he with his hands gripping his elbows, eyes squeezed shut while water bounced heedlessly about, oblivious to how she had to duck and bob to keep the spray out of her face. Damn, had no one taught this priest the rules, the simple *courtesies* of shared showering? She started to laugh, but caught herself when she saw how miserable he looked. Back, she ordered, and pushed him against the wall. The soap was Irish Spring, hinting mischievously of men's colognes and skin bracers—a secret life? Whipping up a lather she first did his neck, then his back, (Turn!) his chest—carefully along the raw-looking scar—then under his arms—he flinched, he was ticklish—all in workmanlike fashion. Turn again! And all the time he continued to cringe, his outsized hands hanging in midair, eyelids buried shut. Both arms, the hands, squeezing their girth as she rubbed, squeezing the webs too between his fingers. Then his buttocks, his thighs, making him raise each leg over hers so she could do his calves and feet, again rubbing carefully in the webs between his toes. Then, only then, did she acknowledge with her soapy hands his rather hangdog erection, carefully—the skin around his scrotum was still yellow-green from the surgery.

And then rose up on her toes and embraced him and enclosed him between her thighs. And in that one swift move under the silky flesh of the water put flesh to her dream, invading his mouth with her tongue and probing, probing until she felt the heat of his anus around her finger. And so they remained. And sometime in the midst of the warm orchestral thudding she heard him sigh.

It was by far the longest shower she had ever experienced. Later she realized one can hope for such an endless supply of hot water only in major league apartments and hotels, settings far beyond her present budget, but well within her dreams, for someday, she was certain, Jonathan and she would routinely shower in such luxury, and secretly she would always think back to this, the first time—rebellious, irreverent thoughts—the kind she had long since discovered would buzz through her head as she sat in the hushed and sacred presence of the dying, holding the patient's hand—as she sat now holding Father Julian's hand until he fell asleep—or so she thought. The moment she withdrew to leave he opened his eyes.

What, she said.

He waved his hand, almost negligently, the way he had dismissed an article of clothing or one of his paintings; then turned his head away.

She closed the door softly behind her.

The next morning he was found dead by the visiting nurse and everyone agreed it was just what he would have wanted—to die in his sleep. And that night she drew Jonathan under the water with her, letting him comfort her and kiss her tears. He understood. Such a good man, such a good man, so very sad. Whispering they soaped each other the way they had always done. Jonathan was first rate in the shower. Only a few more years, he promised. Then he would feel ready to start a family. A few more years of subbing, that's all. And she agreed, she had to agree, that was not too much to ask. Under the comforting water they continued to soap each other, planning their future. And as the water started to turn cold she realized that Father Julian would never know—perhaps it was just as well—and now it was too late to tell him. Art is short. It is life, *life* that is long.

Devotion

Right from the start I figured he was going to be a problem. The way he watched me. Hovered over everything I did. So much devotion. Sometimes they have so much they never want to give up. It's pathetic really—it almost always ends up bad.

I could understand though—it was his wife. Deirdre Ames. Forty-three. Must have been her fourth or fifth trip to the ICU. I could tell—any nurse could tell—it was going to be her last. Metastatic breast cancer. The chemotherapy and bone marrow transplant had done their best. And their worst. And left her what she was now—this bald skeleton hooked up to a respirator. What she was once, I would guess, was really really pretty.

He kept saying: *Do everything. Do everything. You heard me. Do everything.*

Like he was trying to get back at life for what it had done to him. It made him into not a very nice man. But then in this place you got to make allowances. You don't get to see people on their best days. A CEO for one of those techie companies. CEO-handsome—you know what I mean. Chin dimple. Teeth whitener. CEO voice, you know what I mean. Looked like he worked out regularly. Roger was his name only I called him Mr. Ames of course. He'd come in around lunchtime. Always brought this bunch of roses. Every day. Got them in the gift shop. Fresh red roses. Obviously he loved her. Just couldn't let go.

Word was he'd shopped around for the most aggressive oncologist until he found Dr. Gruber. Oh yeah, Dr. Gruber was his man. All us nurses knew Dr. Gruber. Always strutting around elbows out like one of those coaches you see on TV. Always saying: *We're going full court press.* That was his favorite expression when any of us asked what the heck were we doing. *Full court press, we're going full court press.*

He was the one who suckered her into the bone marrow transplant. Which only made her more miserable. Transplants are no use for metastatic breast cancer. That's what all the studies showed when they finally got around to doing them. More time in the hospital, more infections, more pain. Any nurse could have told you that all along. Anyway, after going through all that she still was full of cancer.

But I remember thinking what can you do. It's devotion.

Then there was this other guy. He was kind of a puzzle. I hardly ever saw him because he usually came in only later at night when Cynthia was on. He'd be in and out very quickly. We couldn't figure him exactly, a good friend or brother or something. Blond guy. Quiet. Not much for looks. In the movies, you know, he'd be the bad-luck character. Say a few lines and get shot. Cynthia told me he'd just sit there next to her for a few minutes. Then when he got up to go he'd lean over the bottom of the bed—and Cynthia swore this was true—and kiss her foot. That's not what a brother would do I said to Cynthia and she agreed.

As for Mr. Ames—Roger—he didn't just sit there. No way. Always bouncing up and down, wiggling and checking her IV's and tubes, flipping through her chart. Always insisting we do another X-ray or an MRI or something, anything to show we weren't giving up. Every day he made us stick her to check on her electrolytes.

You heard me. Do everything.

As for me I never could move fast enough for him. When an IV needle got plugged up I tried fiddling with it because it was hard to find a good vein and I hated to keep sticking her. But that didn't suit him. *Pull it out,* he'd say. *And get a new IV going. Right now!*

And I never suctioned her often enough. You could see the way it made her gag and retch and I tried to tell him it was more than she really needed. But that only made him madder.

He said he was going to report me to Dr. Gruber.

Still that's what devotion does I figured. It's awful but it's human. And let's face it we're only human. We can't stand to see the people we love die. I try to keep that in mind. Otherwise you burn out pretty fast. Between people like Mr. Ames who keep hoping for a miracle and doctors like Dr. Gruber who think they've always got one up their sleeve, life in the ICU can get pretty grim, not just for patients.

Finally I had enough though. I called for an ethics consult. That always makes Dr. Gruber mad and it sure made Mr. Ames mad. But that was all I could do. In our hospital the rule is anyone can call for an ethics consult.

At the meeting was Dr. Gruber, Mr. Ames, me, and the ethics consult Dr. Morrison. He insisted we call him Doctor Morrison, only he wasn't a real doctor he was a Ph.D. philosopher. There we were in this crowded little exam room, around the exam table with all these cabinets packed with instruments and medical supplies and not enough chairs. I had to sit on the sink.

Dr. Morrison asked why I had called for a consult.

"Mrs. Ames is miserable." I said. "Even when she's just lying there you can see she's in pain. And it's only worse when we turn her. Everything we do makes her suffer. We all know she's dying. Why can't we just let her die in peace?"

Dr. Morrison scowled and pursed his lips the way I guess philosophers are taught to do to show how carefully they're analyzing a problem. "How do you know she's in pain," he says. "Did the patient herself tell you in so many words she's in pain?"

And I thought to myself Jeezus H why don't you just go in and look at her. But all I said was. "She can't talk. If she didn't have an endo-trache tube in her she'd be screaming."

"Does she have a legally signed advance directive?"

"No," I said. He knows as well as I do almost no one does.

"Well then, who is her surrogate decision maker?"

"I am," says Mr. Ames glaring at me. "I'm her husband."

"So then." says Dr. Morrison. "The patient's husband is exercising the patient's autonomy in his capacity as her surrogate decision maker." Which seemed to clear up the problem for him and he turned to Mr. Ames and this time he really scowled and pursed his lips. "What do *you* think she would want?"

"She would want you to do everything," says Mr. Ames. "I'm sure of it."

"She's always trying to pull out her feeding tube," I said but Dr. Morrison ignored me.

Dr. Gruber chimed in. "I myself asked Mr. Ames here did he want a full court press. Yes he said. And I said You mean all heroic measures? And he said Yes. Definitely. *All heroic measures.*"

And I thought to myself, Jeezus H what a crappy concept. *Heroic measures.* These people think flogging this poor woman is heroic. Death is coming! Call in the Machines! Like they're brave soldiers about to be overrun by the enemy. Call in the bombers! Except for those guys, being heroic meant being willing to die. No. The way I figure it these people are anything but heroic. Just the opposite. They're *afraid* to die.

But Dr. Gruber was looking right at me even as he was talking to Mr. Ames. "Correct me if I'm wrong, Mr. Ames," he says. "But aren't those our exact words?"

And of course Mr. Ames says Yes, those were the exact words.

Still, Dr. Morrison had to be philosophically certain. "What you're saying if I understand you correctly, Mr. Ames, is that you yourself, exercising your authority as surrogate decision-maker for Mrs. Ames, told Dr. Gruber your wife would want every possible life-sustaining measure employed to keep her alive. Is that what you're saying?"

"*Yes, it is*," he says with that CEO voice of his that meant he expected it to be done snappily and that's final.

And I could see that that was going to be it, end of ethics consult. Which meant I'd have to hurry if I wanted to get a few words in. I mean I've been there before. *Do everything*, the family says, all teary eyed, and like Mr. Ames they go home to sleep. And the doctors? "You heard them," the doctors always say as they sweep by on rounds with their noses buried in the medical charts. "*Do everything.*" Far as they're concerned if the electrolytes check out they've done their job. Meanwhile we're left with the patient.

So I'm used to it. I try whenever I can to spot when maybe the family is beginning to see the light. Sometimes I even get to say the words. "Look," I say. "Don't we all want to die in our sleep? Isn't that what we hope for in the end?" And they look at me. And sometimes the look is relief. Like it's what they've been thinking all along, only they didn't know it was okay to think that way. Of course sometimes the look isn't all that friendly. You got to be careful. So I tell them, "What I'm saying is you won't change *that* she's going to die, all you're going to do is change *how* she's going to die."

Those were the words I tried to slip in before Dr. Morrison took out his pen to write his little philosophical note in the chart. And even though I was only the nurse on the case I'd been there so many times I just couldn't keep my mouth shut. I let them have it. Not many nurses are willing to do this but I couldn't stand it any more. "Look," I said. And I guess I sort of got carried away. "Instead of letting Mrs. Ames die in peace," I said, "what we're doing to her means she'll spend her last miserable days in pain. Drowning in all the fluids we're pumping into her body. Until she finally throws up and chokes on whatever we've stuck in her useless stomach. That is if she doesn't have a cardiac arrest first. And because she's Full Code that means we're not going to let her go without pounding on her chest and shocking her and breaking her ribs and..."

At that Mr. Ames stands up and says, "*I want this nurse removed from the case.*"

And I said, "*That's what your heroic measures are doing.*"

And Dr. Gruber got up and said he would see to it.

You can see why nurses don't last long in the ICU. Not that I was all that worried about getting fired or anything. Who would they get to replace me? The hospital is going nuts trying to find qualified ICU nurses. Well think about it. Who wants to put up with all that crap? Especially now with HMO downsizing and re-engineering and all those crappy words that mean the stockholders get more for their money and the patients get less? They couldn't find another nurse like me if they tried. It just meant that Cynthia and me had to change sections and overlap shifts until Mrs. Ames died, which we all knew she would.

As for Dr. Gruber no one ever dies. They suffer a cardiac arrest. No one's got terminal pneumonia. You just got to goose up the respirator. No one's got kidney failure. They just need dialysis. And so on. Oh, and go light on the morphine. Don't want to turn them into addicts. Over the years I've seen nurses quit right on the spot because they couldn't stand what he did to his patients. Either that or slip them a little extra morphine, you know what I mean. Something I'd never done. Only I can't say I never thought about it. We even have a joke about him. Question: Why do they put heavy concrete slabs on top of graves? Answer: To keep out Dr. Gruber.

But I suppose patients get the doctors they deserve. Or so I thought.

Anyway, the schedule shift meant I got to see this other visitor, the blond guy, and Cynthia was right. He just sat there next to her for a few minutes, didn't try to talk to her or anything, and when he left sure enough he really did bend down and kiss her foot. I thought she was asleep but just to be sure I looked in after he left and sort of whispered: *Everything all right?* Naturally I was afraid the guy was some kind of wierdo. To my surprise Mrs. Ames nodded. Pretty definitely. Like she really was all right. She couldn't speak, of course, what with the endotrache tube and all. But—well, she didn't seem any worse off having had her foot kissed.

Anyway, as you can guess I couldn't help having my suspicions about what was going on. And sure enough it all became clear when Mrs. Ames finally had her cardiac arrest. I heard the Code Blue on the intercom and hurried over to see. There he was standing right there by the door. Mr. Ames. Waving the code team and the crash cart into the room. Waving, waving. *Get in there!* And they start their pounding and shocking and blasting air and pumping her chest. And I see him standing outside listening to all that racket with what seemed to me satisfaction.

And I suddenly had a completely new take on devotion. It wasn't devotion. It was revenge.

Harry And The Girl

Harry didn't notice the young girl at first. Not that he didn't remember her, her face particularly, fruit-tart bright with acne, her dreary eyes—he had seen her there many times in the waiting room, unlit cigarette stuck between her fingers, wilting sullenly in the corner amid the tropical-fish tanks, sectional couches, and racks containing health brochures.

This was the one who kept trying to kill herself. (Twice while lying cold and half-naked on the slick white butcher paper, Harry had heard Dr. Ackerman in the next exam room pleading exasperatedly, first with her then on the phone with the psychiatrist.)

Smeary hair and faded jeans, ratty T-shirt—featuring this time something in Italian—costume bracelet, and thongs that exposed young soiled delicate toes. Harry didn't realize he was staring at her toes until she suddenly yanked her feet under her.

"How we doing," said Harry.

Nothing. A silent smirking nemesis. The same thing every time: Harry made a point of smiling, tried to engage her in polite conversation—it used to make Rose jealous—but the girl never said a word.

When the nurse called her in, two women shook their heads.

"Takes all kinds," said the one wearing a blue machine-washable stretch pantsuit that suggested chartered bus trips and art museum tours.

"Not much you can do," acknowledged the other, a heavyset woman in a billowy orange-red dress.

The girl was well known to the other patients. A character. Stories abounded. Everyone heard how she had turned the gas on in her apartment one Sunday and nearly blown up the whole building. More than once Harry had seen her in the waiting room with both wrists bandaged. And the things she swallowed were legendary: not only the usual aspirin tablets and tranquilizers, but shoe polish, cough syrup, bleach, contact lens cleaner, calamine lotion, tie dye, all her dermatologicals; she had even tried gobbling down lipstick.

On those days she had burst into Dr. Ackerman's waiting room, her face and mouth

clownishly painted, heaving up broths that
defied description and could still be seen, indel-
ibly fixed to his Scandinavian carpet. There
would be the usual disaster drill with people
shouting and taking cover, Dr. Ackerman
would be on the phone to the psychiatrist and
everyone's appointment would be delayed
even more than usual.

She was a depressive, of course; everyone
agreed, although naturally they debated
whether her efforts were serious or merely gestures to gain attention.

"Every night, I look for her on the evening
news," said the pantsuited woman.

"Least she could do is wash her clothes," said
the heavyset woman "if she can't fix her face."

Pantsuit agreed people should take better
care of themselves, only what with drugs and
all they're all too busy, aren't they.

Harry intervened. "I had it bad too when I
was a kid," he said. "Acne. Miserable stuff."

But the heavyset woman wasn't buying
it. You don't go around blowing up people
because you got acne, she pointed out. Her
reddish orange dress had gigantic wiggles and
splotches, all very modernistic and fashionable, and wrong for her, thought Harry. But
Harry forgave her for that. He knew how hard
it was to keep the spirits up.

He himself had entered the world today in
designer-monogrammed burgundy socks he

had washed the night before and Adidas which made his feet look young and playful, fortifying himself further with madras shirt, Daks slacks, wire-framed bifocal fashion glasses, beige Members Only jacket with sporty shoulder epaulets, and a jaunty, not too ostentatious silvery toupee.

"Thing is," said Harry, "if it were anything but a face, you'd call it beautiful, wouldn't you." The women looked at him. "I mean the colors and all." They lofted their eyebrows at each other.

The nurse appeared. "Harry," she called.

Dr. Ackerman was lean and tan; only his salmon-colored, blow-dried hair seemed to have any flesh to it. On the walls of the examining rooms were poster-size photographs of him running in marathons.

"So how we doing, Harry?" he said, then held his finger up to shush him until he had finished listening to his heart. "Super. Let's get dressed." He leafed through Harry's record. "Last time we were walking six blocks."

"What for?"

"So how many can we do now? Before we get chest pain."

Harry shrugged. "The real hell of it is I can't make it up the ladder, can't pick the apricots at the top of my little tree anymore." Harry gave a surly laugh. "Story of my life."

Dr. Ackerman waited, his slim gold pen poised. "I need a number."

"Apricots?"

"Blocks. Helps me keep track."

Harry shrugged. He had no idea how many blocks he walked now. Now he took buses. Now he traveled not blocks, but hours. Now he consumed not space, but time. Hours. Days. Now the point of moving was not to go from one place to another, but from sunrise to sunset. A trip to the beach used up an hour and twenty minutes, a trip to the downtown Horton Plaza including a movie, most of the afternoon. Shopping could be counted on for maybe two hours if he missed connections. He called them adventures, but the truth was nothing ever happened. Not like the old days. Now he always seems to be waiting. For something, anything, to take him away from this place to that place, from where he was to someplace else. Waiting the way Rose waited, eyes hobbled by pain, pointed at death—each time Dr. Ackerman had come up with a new drug that kept it loping back and forth just out of reach—and sometimes as he waited and remembered, a whimper would escape him right there at the bus stop. Dr. Ackerman's voice brought him back, not unkindly.

"So. We taking our Prozac, Harry?"

Harry shook his head.

"How about exercise?"

"What's wrong with that girl?"

"What girl?"

"You know the one I mean. Keeps trying to bump herself off."

Dr. Ackerman shrugged.

"*Help* her, for Chrissake!"

"What can I do? I can't take her pills for her." Dr. Ackerman laughed, patted him on the back. "You're almost as bad as she is, you know that? Just kidding."

The nurse buzzed. Dr. Ackerman was falling behind.

Harry reached for his shirt. "Why do you keep this place so damn cold?" He buttoned hastily, irritably. "Sleeping pills. That's what I should be taking. One big bunch of sleeping pills."

"Harry." Dr. Ackerman sighed. "Harry, Harry..."

The young girl was waiting downstairs in the pharmacy. "Didn't hurt you too bad, did he?" Harry said cheerily. "Me, he gave a heart transplant. That's what took so long, but I'll be okay. Just kidding."

The girl smirked and said nothing. She picked up her little brown paper bag of medicine. Harry nodded agreeably as she went by. "Prozac, right? How about a little Prozac, he said."

The girl had twisted past him with such force he thought she would be miles away by the time he got his refills. But there she was, right there at the bus stop, smoking, squinting in the glare of the buildings and store windows.

"Well, look at that," he said. "I thought nobody but me rode the bus in this town."

She didn't answer.

He shifted the bag in his hands a few times. "Back where I grew up, Chicago, everybody rode the bus. Some nights you even got your tuxedoes and evening gowns."

He shifted the bag, waited.

"You meet people, talk to people."

He shifted the bag, waited.

"Wife and me, Rosie, we used to take the bus all the time."

He shifted the bag, waited.

"I used to bring her to Dr. Ackerman."

The girl flopped her bag sharply. "I seen her," she said, finally.

"Hey, what do you know," said Harry. "She walks, she talks. Where you headed?"

The girl shrugged.

"What's that mean?" He shrugged back.

"Home."

"Home? What's at home? What do you say we go to the beach?" The girl looked at him, and even Harry couldn't believe what he had just done. He had just asked her on a date.

"Where's your wife," the girl said.

"What do you mean where's my wife?" Harry revived vocal resonances he hadn't called upon in decades. "What's it to you where my wife is? Am I asking you to marry me?" Harry laughed. "Hey, here it comes. We transfer to the Number 34 and it'll get us to Mission Beach." The girl hesitated. "Come on, come on. I'll treat, don't worry."

Except for them the bus was empty.

"See what I mean?" He stood in the aisle and waved his arms in the air like an orchestra conductor calling for more volume. Put his hand to his ear. Nothing. "And they call it public transportation." He wheeled around, one hand holding onto the seat handle, the other—the one with the brown paper bag, which admittedly undermined the gallantry of the gesture—offering her the window.

But the girl had already brushed past him, sat down and stared straight ahead, making odd faces every now and then to stretch her rash. She reached up to scratch her hair, first shaking down her bracelets. Harry noticed the little white scars on her wrist.

"Know something?" he said, settling down next to her. "That piece there is jade, you know. And real copper. Don't make costume jewelry like that anymore." The girl shrugged. "I used to own my own jewelry business. Harry's Jewelry. You probably heard of it." He looked at her, tried a twinkle in his eye. Nothing. "You got a job?"

"No."

"How come?"

"How come? Because! That's how come."

"Because what? You do *something* don't you?"

"I don't do *nothing*. That's what I do." Again she flapped her bag, signifying end of subject.

Harry massaged the bag in his lap, taking comfort for a moment in its responsive crackle. "You know what Rosie did? Played the oboe. That's how I met her. My first concert. Ever been to one of those? I don't mean one of your dinky rock things. I mean eighty, a hundred people up there playing all at once. In the middle I hear this—I don't know—this sound, you know, like there's this like *bird* flying way out over the ocean, and I see this little woman playing this like stick of a thing. I'll never forget that sound. And I said to the guy next to me, 'What's that?' I said." Harry leaned forward to check the bus stop, then leaned back. "And he says to me, 'That? That's an oboe.' And I said, 'Hey, I gotta meet that oboe.'"

Harry waited, but the girl didn't speak. Another stop. "Almost there, he said. "Six months later we got married. Pretty quick work for those days. So how come you don't got a job?"

"Because, I said."

"Because what? Because you got acne?"

"Fuck off!"

"I had the worst acne you ever saw."

"I'm not *interested* in your acne."

Harry let go of the bag and rubbed his hands surreptitiously on his pants. They left little sweat marks.

"Anyway, coming out here was my idea. Let's get some sunshine, I said. Wait a minute, here's where we switch to the Number 34. Look at that, we're in luck. Here it comes."

Harry got up and turned to the girl who remained seated. "Come on, come on." He waved the transfers. "Alright, I'm sorry. I won't talk about my acne anymore. Come on."

"What for?"

"Why not? Why not, why *not?*" He nearly shouted.

The argument seemed persuasive. The girl made a face but got up.

The Number 34 bus turned toward the ocean, first entering its own seething sea of cars, along Rosecrans Street and Midway Drive, past drive-ins and discount stores, plumbing suppliers and TV renters, past glittery car-covered parking lots, before proceeding along Mission Boulevard. Harry waited for the girl to say something, but all he heard was the shuffling sounds of traffic, the groaning of the bus, all of it merging with the smoky sourness of the air, all of it oppressively familiar, like the taste of his digestive juices.

"Listen," he said, finally. "I gotta tell you something. I don't like the look on your face."

"Fuck off."

"I don't mean the acne, that's not what I mean. I mean you got that look—you know who had that look? Rosie had that look. That *look*."

"Fuck off."

"Fuck off. Fuck off." Harry shook his head at her. "I'm really disappointed that's all you got to say, you know that?" Then he turned toward the window. Christ, the whole place was a disappointment. What did they say nowadays? A downer, a *real downer*. Everything held together with aluminum strips and fiberboard. Insubstantial. Like a disease to which even the hardy Rose succumbed. He dismissed the scene with a wave of his hand. "Stuff wouldn't last one night in Chicago. One puff off the lake." He looked back at her. "What makes you think you got a *right*? You haven't even *lived!*"

"Fuck *off*," she hissed. "Fuck off fuck off fuck *off!*"

"Oh, listen to that. Shock the geezer. Right? Listen, you want to know shocking? Me and Rosie, you know what we used to do? We used to go riding on my motorcycle with no clothes on." Harry laughed and wiped his mouth. "And I mean Rosie did too, that girl. We go roaring along, our fannies squashed together on the seat. Old geezers looking out the windows, by the time they figured out what was happening— phew!—we were gone!"

The girl jumped up and pushed her way past him. Aah. Shit. What had he done? Harry pulled himself out of the seat and stumbled after her. "Okay, okay, I'm sorry. I got carried away." He looked out through the driver's windows. They had reached the water. Ahead lay the scaly dazzle of the beach. The sky a hazy blue like galvanized siding. The bus driver glanced over at them and Harry nodded a brief reassuring smile before they got off. He felt he owed him that. People get all sorts of ideas.

The sidewalk was jammed with strollers, surfers, people on skateboards, bicycles, roller skates—a glowing muscular swarm into which the girl instantly plunged.

He trotted after her. "Listen, I said I'm sorry."

Without stopping the girl looked over her shoulder, flipped her hair. Her face twitched. "Get the fuck away from me, will you."

"I *said* I'm sorry."

"I'll call the cops, man."

"Look," Harry pleaded in a low voice. They were bumped apart. He caught up. "Things happen. Things happen you never expect." Again she tossed her head as though trying to shake him off. "Okay, okay. I'm a pain in the ass. You think I don't know that? But listen. You want to hear something? The night Rosie dies I come home from the hospital and I swear

Tosca—that's our dog—I swear she *knows.* You know what she does?"

"Fuck off."

"She climbs up and from then on she sleeps in the bed with me. You think that's weird? Well, I'll tell you something. It's nice. Warm. That's what I mean. Things happen, things you never expect, things you never imagine... Shit."

The girl had vaulted the concrete seawall and was headed for the water. Harry looked for the stairs; by the time he hit the sand he was way behind her. His Adidas sank and skidded. Meanwhile the girl swept through the swarm of bodies like a swift darkness, an avenging angel.

"Wait..." Harry gasped, his breath cloyed by lotions and barbecues. Deep in his chest he heard the first faint call of a distant bird.

Fully clothed the girl splashed into the water.

"Wait a minute, for Chrissake..." Harry hesitated, looked around at the astonished expressions of pot-bellied men and women with bruised white legs gingerly poised at the water's edge. "Shit," he announced and plunged in after her.

He managed to grab hold of her arm when a huge wave threw her back. She kicked and scratched and Harry found himself underwater clinging to her legs and for a moment he was aware of toes flicking deliciously through his fingers, like a trill accompanying the melancholy song in his chest.

Now they were rising up, craning their necks, gasping for air, now they were going under again. Harry was hanging on to her T-shirt, and this frail handful of cotton rather than his feet became his anchor. So this is death, Harry thought as he swirled and swatted clumsily, comically, as the trilling sound mocked him, soared, now a kind of high-pitched riveting in his body. This is death, he thought and at that very moment Harry felt a percussive force possess him from behind. Do your work swiftly, he begged, closed his eyes and waited.

Then opened them again and saw his toupee floating next to him like a hairy jellyfish and felt himself being pulled back.

And Harry realized with a tinge of regret that he was being rescued.

On the beach the two of them were surrounded by a flock of bathers, like fleshy predatory creatures all in a blur. He reached up to fix the blur, discovered his glasses were gone.

"You want us to call a cop or something," a voice was saying close to his ear, and Harry realized he was being held with his arm behind his back.

Harry waited. It seemed an eternity. The girl's eyes veered, then leveled, found the range, settled on him. "Just tell him to fuck off," she said with only the briefest shake of her head, barely acknowledging his presence.

"You heard her," someone said.

"Creep," someone else said, and he was released and pushed away.

Harry squished through the jostling crowd as quickly as he could, hesitating only for a moment when he heard a voice, "You need some help?" But they were talking to the girl.

Not until he had cleared the seawall and merged with the crowd of strollers on the sidewalk did he dare turn around and look back. The bathers were still gathered. Somewhere in their midst, he knew, was the young girl. Meanwhile around him people were staring. Sopping wet, fully clothed, he was clutching what he realized was not his bag of medicine, but his toupee. He moved on, squishing.

When the bus stopped the driver held up his hand. For a moment Harry was afraid he wouldn't let him board. But Harry managed to dig exact change out of his wet pants and wave back—two men, hands aloft, engaged in an exotic tribal ritual. The bus driver nodded and Harry went straight to the rear.

And there he sat and for the first time allowed himself to give way to what had happened. He couldn't believe it. An adventure. It had happened. To him. His clothes, clinging and chill left no doubt. It was true what he told the girl. All sorts of things happen, things you'd never expect, things you'd never imagine. And now he became aware, before he became unaware, that the song in his chest, a pain really, was singing with a strange distant compelling elation.

The Passover War

Anyway, he couldn't believe it. Me, this *shiksa* from Sonoma State knew more about the high holidays than he did. But, there you go—while he had been busy repressing his childhood, all my Jewish boyfriends were getting their kicks out of bringing me home for Passover Seder. Me, this "Nazi." (I grew up in Laguna Beach, but I'm one of those skinny long-legged blondes, you know, and my name is Christina.)

"You've been to Seders?" Michael said. He laughed and almost spilled his coffee. It was our first date, a cafe in Jerusalem. The music, believe it or not, was the Bee Gees.

And the look on his face made me laugh, too. His eyes behind his glasses so startled. He rubbed his nose like he had been hit. Hurt, almost. Like he was expecting a virgin and I just told him I did porno movies. (Actually, I

L . J . S c h n e i d e r m a n

did do one. Hadn't gotten around to telling him, though.)

"Even did a Seder on an Apache reservation," I boasted. (That isn't all we did. This weird med student and his friend in the Indian Health Service cooked up some peyote and we ended up doing a rain dance. In the rain.)

I caught Michael looking at me uneasily. Uh oh, reverse engines. Coming on too strong. Didn't want the evening to be totaled before it even got started. (Actually, it was just one of those twenty-five-cent peep show things—got fifty bucks for playing with myself and anyway, all that stuff's in the past.) Not that I was all that crazy about him yet. But it was a relief to find an American for a change. All that swaggering prickly charm of Israeli men had pretty much worn thin for me.

Also, there was this nice feeling of predestination. Okay, coincidence. But it made for what we used to call good karma, remember? (Ah yes, the good old days!) The morning he started working in the TV repair shop was the morning I'd decided I'd had it with my old black and white, the picture running up or down at the slightest disturbance—like eating an egg salad sandwich in the same room.

"So, a sensitive one," Michael said when I brought it in. I liked the way he touched it, ran his hand across it.

Pretty soon we were talking. He had already applied for Israeli citizenship. As for me, I had no intention of staying past the summer, when my grant ran out.

"What are you into?" he said. Christ, can you imagine? I hadn't heard my native tongue in months.

"Ethnomethodology," I said. "Only I'm not into jargon anymore. So I'm typing up my field notes so I can collect my last paycheck so I can get the hell out."

Michael was looking at me—I remember his eyes, even from the beginning, small but intense, like these two bees in a bottle. "Later, you want to have coffee or something," he said.

I don't know how we got started talking about the Jewish holidays. To get anything out of him took a bit of digging, probing as we say.

"I celebrated Hanukah once around a Christmas tree," I told him. "My boyfriend's father lit the menorah candles dressed as Santa Claus. How about you?"

The cafe was smoky and noisy; waiters kept squeezing around us, dropping spoons, spilling coffee. I didn't always catch what he said, but I could see I had scratched a raw nerve or something.

"Hanukah?" he said, making a face and rubbing his nose again. My father wouldn't even touch Hanukah. Jews who inflated this minor holiday to compete with Christmas were *traif,* he said. You understand Yiddish? No?" Michael waved his hand. "Neither do I. That's one of the three words I know. The other two I forgot. Garbage. Crap. Something like that."

That was the first I heard about Michael's father. Tell the truth, I got to know more about him than about Michael. It seemed the old man dealt with Christmas like, you know, Macy's, Saks, and Neiman Marcus—making sure he was there to catch some of the money we crazy *goyim* threw away on it. Pincus Cohen. A pious Jew, a leader in the synagogue, elder, in a place called Flatbush. He was a printer— so for him it was personalized Christmas cards, complete with those toothpasty photographs. He composed them with a kind of diabolical glee—elaborate gothic type and all that high fashion crap, fancy curlicues, strange colors. And naturally, because he made a point of charging more than twice the going rate, he picked up a substantial clientele. Was I angry at all at this? Michael asked. No. Why should I be? I replied. To be fleeced like that by a Jew was the story of my people. Right from the beginning. J.C. of Biblical fame. Look what that bastard did.

Another nose rub. I don't think he expected that kind of talk from me. Me, Miss Surfing U.S.A.

"The thing he hated most about me was that I let the print shop 'pass away'. His only son."

"He *hated* you?"

"It's mutual."

"Your only father."

"The thing is he wouldn't let me touch anything. Printing for him was an act of manhood. Like wearing a yarmulke."

"That too?"

"That too. He wouldn't let me wear one at a Seder until I 'grew up,' you know."

"Is that kosher? I mean aren't all boys supposed to wear those things?"

"In the synagogue, yes. In his own house he was a *Halukah* unto himself. One year I was set to do the Four Questions. In Hebrew. From memory. But at the last minute I disappointed him. Got bad grades, maybe. Lost something. Who knows? All I know is he gave the job to one of my cousins. A girl. Younger than me. And wouldn't let me wear a yarmulke. It was very humiliating. Why am I telling you this?"

We both laughed and finished our coffee without looking at each other.

"You want to go for a walk or something?" said Michael.

I moved in with him a week or so later. With the understanding that it was only temporary, of course. Michael's room was right over some shops in a noisy part of the city. The *Machnea Yehuda*, the old marketplace. The apartment itself looked new. He told me it had just been put back together after a suicide bomber had killed the previous tenant. Also killed were the tenant's mynah bird, a Carthusian monk and an old Arab woman. (I was nervous. Sleeping there the first few nights. Not by what the bomb had done—and might do again—actually, but what the bomb had said, you know what I mean? I mean what was the point of killing the bird for Chrissake—I don't know, it's hard to describe).

Anyway, by the time I met Michael I was already homesick. There we were entertaining each other with American expressions like, "What're you into?" "To the max." "Chill out." "Hey man, what's happening?" and stuff like that. And the greatest treat of all would be not going out to the movies, but just staying home and cooking up hamburgers. Sometimes we'd watch television (Michael wouldn't let me hit it anymore). Sometimes we'd walk.

Usually on these walks I'd do some more probing. Michael was part of an extended family, the kind you read about, but never see anymore—uncles, aunts, cousins, nieces, nephews. At the top, running the show, was his father. That is, until Michael came along. Michael was the first one actually to go places the New

York subways didn't go. Which didn't sit too well with the old man. When Michael decided he wanted to study engineering at Purdue, his father practically threw him out of the house. And once sprung he never returned. He was like Moses. Within a few months a whole flock of relatives—cousins, even a few aunts and uncles—took off after him. They'd had it too.

After Purdue, Michael just kept going west until he found a job in electronics south of San Francisco. It wasn't long before he was driving a Porsche, rafting in white water, sleeping with flight attendants and attending Martin Buber seminars—with other mostly unmarried engineers.

It was the Six Day War that brought Michael to Israel. He flew across as soon as he could, but by the time he arrived, the war was over. He had missed it, but stayed anyway. He didn't want to miss the next one, he said.

The summer ended, my grant ran out, it was already into the fall, I kept putting off my return. The truth is I felt good with Michael. A physical feeling? You bet. But, even deeper. Physics. As though the way he was shaped, his chunky darkness had formed a chemical bond with my blonde skinniness. His silence with my jumpiness. His patience—how can I describe it?—he treated me like his television sets, with hands that knew just how to touch me. We had our disagreements of course, but Michael was amazing, always the first to reach out and make up. If he was angry, he would slump down in his chair, hunch his shoulders in his brooding silence. But then all of a sudden, he would simply reach out and touch me. What can you do but want to take care of such a man for the rest of your life?

We thought briefly of moving to Haifa, but the more we saw the less we liked "Israel's San Francisco" with its sky made yellow by the Nesher Cement Works. "They made the desert bloom and the sky a desert," Michael said one day. (He's not so bad once he starts talking.) Anyway, the only jobs Michael could find took him out on the road in out-of-the-way Arab villages trying to hustle soft drinks he wouldn't drink himself or auto parts they couldn't afford. Bad enough he had the Army six weeks out of the year. We decided to stay in Jerusalem. The money wasn't much, and he was always fighting with his boss, but there was a chance he could buy into the store.

We had been living together for almost a year when it happened. I came home from the clinic. "We have to make a decision," I said.

Michael, in his underpants, put down the magazine he was reading. His fingers went right to his nose and started rubbing. Not even noon and it was already hot in our apartment. Summertime. Instead of breeze, the noise and smell of worn-out engines came through the windows. It was as though everything outside was frying—buses, people, buildings, everything sputtering out there in the streets. Even the little plastic radio Michael had on was crackling, frying the news. Michael tried to find a way to relax and as he moved I could hear his hot skin sticking to the chair.

I sat down next to him. My hands, folding and unfolding. I realized while I was hurrying home that I was both happy and frightened. It was because my happiness had rested on untested assumptions, assumptions I had never checked with Michael. I found I couldn't say anything.

"You want to keep it?" he said finally.

"Yes. You?"

"Of course."

(Of course!)

"Then it's settled," I said, almost whimpering with relief.

"Except..."

"I know."

"You'll live here?" Michael asked.

"Of course."

(Of course!)

"Then that's settled, too," said Michael and he jumped up from the chair, lifted me off my feet and laughed a long laugh that I thought would never end. It was almost as though his face had delivered a great burden, had undergone a sudden shifting of cargo, become a different set of bulges and hollows. That laugh took over his whole body—chin, nose, ears, shoulders. A proud father, I thought.

"We should get married," I reminded him.

Michael agreed.

"Back home."

A narrowing scowl.

"Laguna Beach," I said. "You'll meet my folks."

"Settled."

"I can meet your family, too. Your father..."

"Some day," said Michael quietly.

The wedding took place in our back yard; in the shade of the sycamore tree I had helped my father plant, amidst bougainvillea, hibiscus and orange blossoms. The sound of the ocean beneath us as we said our vows. Sun and a hundred different perfumes. It was a fantasy I had forgotten about. My long blond relatives in their pastel gowns and eggshell summer suits flowed around Michael, surrounded him; in his compact darkness he looked like a black olive in a punchbowl of champagne. He charmed them all. My mother and father glowing with smiles. I sensed I had fulfilled fantasies of theirs, too (one of their fantasies was that they were liberal). We were married by a Rabbi in a Mexican shirt who played a guitar and sang Hassidic folk songs. (Where did they ever find him?) No sweat about the pregnancy. After

Sonoma State they had braced themselves for anything I suppose. (Almost anything—I never told them about the porno movie. I decided not to tell Michael either.)

As soon as we got back to Israel, Michael arranged to switch the job in his reserve unit to something in communications, something less likely to get him involved in combat. I was grateful for that. Nothing to prove anymore, Michael, I said. Proving had nothing to do with it, he answered, hunching his shoulders.

And then came the war Michael had been waiting for. All through the summer the news was unsettling, drills, false alarms—only the speeches were reassuring. "Dado," our Chief of Staff, and Dayan, our Defense Minister, had everything under control. Intelligence knew Sadat's plans even before he did. True, we were surrounded, but weren't they the same schleppy Arabs who managed to trip over each other all these years? Those same Arabs who herded their women around like animals and pissed in the streets, who told the craziest lies and believed all the crazy ones they were told.

The sirens began at two in the afternoon, Yom Kippur, catching Michael and me while we were quietly making love.

"What is it," Michael shouted out the window to a man he saw running.

The man's reply was lost as he disappeared down the street. Michael quickly got dressed and followed him.

With Michael gone that night I hardly slept. The next morning I got up early—too early for the golden glow of Jerusalem's stone buildings to appear and lift my spirits. Instead, the air was filled with a crackling of transistor radios, the news of the war coming from every window and door and passing car. On the pretense of shopping for the baby I wandered in and out of stores, hardly paying attention to the frocks, the bottles, the teething rings, the packages of diapers that my hands went over numbly before pushing them away. In retrospect I realized I didn't want to be home, didn't want to hear the telephone. I thought if I stayed away it wouldn't ring. So many other women, moving as though in a dream, seemed to be doing the same thing.

But it rang anyway, late that evening as I opened the door. A woman's voice, sympathetic but brisk and practical. She had other calls to make before she too could go home. Michael had just come out of surgery. Although his condition was officially listed as critical, someone had told her she had overheard the doctors talking. They were very pleased. I should come to the hospital and as soon as the doctors had a chance—naturally they were very busy—they would explain things to me.

"Is he going to be all right?"

"A doctor I'm not. Come. Come."

"Can't you even tell me what happened to him?

"Look, what do you want from me? Come already."

When I finally saw the neurosurgeon he said he was very pleased. The brain swelling seemed to be under control, Michael might very well come out of it in good shape. Of course they would go back in soon to replace the missing fragments of skull with a metal plate. All this in a voice that could have been telling me how he would fix a leak under the sink.

During those first few days I could do no more than sit beside Michael's bed, hold his hand while he slept, and stare at his face, swollen and discolored with bruises, his nose where he rubbed it scraped raw, his head covered in a cupola of gauze. The soldier sent by Michael's unit also said he was very pleased. A lucky man, Michael. Their bus, rushing to the staging area, had crashed head-on into a truck. Four men were instantly killed. (Later, Michael would say, Four Questions: Why Dov? Why Izzy? Why Shimshon? Why Moshe?) The injured were immediately transferred to another bus that was on its way back to Jerusalem to pick up more men. The bus delivered them right away to Hadassah Hospital, saving all their lives.

At last the Egyptian Third Army was surrounded and the war ground to a halt. I phoned Michael's parents.

I told them the doctors were very pleased.

"Who are you?" an old man's querulous voice interrupted.

"I'm Christina."

"Christina?" The disbelief in his voice was unmistakable. Could such a thing, a Christina, even exist?

"We're going to have a baby," I said. "The next time we come to America we'll visit you."

"You're going to visit us?"

"Okay?"

"Don't do us any favors."

On my way to see Michael I stopped off one day to register for a place in the maternity unit. The woman taking the information hesitated when I gave my religion.

"Jewish?" she said.

I explained that I was married in a Jewish ceremony.

"You have conversion papers?"

"Conversion papers?"

The woman left her desk and went through a door. After a few minutes she returned with a man who looked at me with some irritation. He began to ask me questions. Had I studied with a rabbi? Had I been examined by a representative of the Rabbinical Court, done my mikvahs? Where did I get off calling myself a Jew?

Bewildered I asked, "Does this mean I can't have my baby here?"

"Of course not," the man snapped. "In Israel we take care of everybody. Arabs, Jews, Christians, Atheists, Everybody."

"And the baby?"

"That's the rabbi's business. Talk to a rabbi." The man tried to make me feel better. "Why such a long nose? We'll take care of you. We take care of everybody, don't we?"

Michael's recovery continued. For a while he had seizures, but soon these stopped with medicine. Then for a while he had terrible headaches, but then these too stopped, or at least became tolerable, with more medicine. Miraculously, his brain, swaddled in its mound of gauze, recovered. He even began to joke when the surgeons and nurses hovered over one spot that wouldn't heal where the plate had been put in. The nurses regularly unrolled the bandages and the doctors periodically probed it. Every now and then, like a moist womb, it gave birth to a small particle, a glistening grain of sand.

"Like monkeys noshing on my fleas," said Michael, as the surgeons picked at him with what seemed like long, silvery fingernails.

And each day, I would watch the expression of the surgeons as they passed Michael on their rounds. I needed assurance that all was going well, an assurance one of them would grant me with a quick, almost absent glance. He had uncovered many brains since Michael's.

Michael, for his part, never let a day go by that he did not put his hand on my great bulge. Together we felt the gathering restlessness inside me.

Reuven.

I laughed aloud when I got a good look at his face all cleaned up. He was like a cartoon of Michael, all the lines and bulges and darkness exaggerated. As soon as I could I had myself wheeled through the hospital to Michael's bed. There we were, both in the hospital at once.

"You know who he looks like?" Michael complained. Yet he also laughed. Somehow, I knew this little Reuven had reduced Michael's obsession to a joke on himself. How could he hate his father, when there he was, lying in my arms, his own creation, ready to tag along after him? A mocking voodoo doll. Together in our wheelchairs, Michael and I went where we could be private. There he put his arm around me as we both watched Reuven grunting for my milk.

What a change Reuven made. Now Michael began to speak almost fondly of his father. And for me the details became clearer—a strawberry patch of scalp spreading apart the old man's wispy gray hair, his sagging belly held up by a thin black monogrammed belt. I could hear the asthmatic wheezes throughout dinner.

Elder of Flatbush. I began to see a man who
did not stand so much as squat, head pushed
forward, eyes blinking, king of the frogs.

Every year Passover began when he
appeared at their apartment door in a new
polyester suit—usually made up of one of those
patterns and colors that end up on discount
racks. The women would shriek adoringly, his
mother along with aunts, nieces and cousins
who trooped in for the ceremonious review
from nearby apartments. That was the signal.
The women and children set to work, purifying
the apartment, making it kosher for *Pesach*, followed by the annual unpacking of the Passover
treasure—china, linen, napkins, glasses, silver.
While his father issued commands, Michael
helped move the mahogany table into the living room, where it stood on its thick legs and
presided, a great banquet table now. The stuffy
apartment began to glitter like a palace. Gone
were the books and magazines that had lain in
heaps on top of tables, chairs, even the floor.
Packed in boxes they were shoved under beds
where relatives slept. In their places appeared
crystal bowls, silver platters, salt and pepper
shakers of all shapes and sizes, bottles of wine
and seltzer water, candlesticks, pitchers, and of
course the great blue and gold Seder plate.

The celebration went on past the two
Seder nights for the full eight days. Michael's
father presided over everything. From the first

shifting of furniture to the last Passover song, Michael's father, elder of Flatbush, lord of his domain, in his shiny suit and silken *yarmulke, presided.*

Michael suddenly became silent.

"Yes?"

Nothing.

"Go on. Please."

"*Mah nishtanah ha-lailah ha-zeh mi-kol ha-lay-lot* ? Why is this night different from all other nights?"

"So you do remember. Tell me."

For years he had dreamed of the night when he would place the silk cap on his head and before the light of the burning candles, in the swimming blue and gold of Passover reflected in the watchful faces, would become one of the men, would utter the mysterious words, the bewitching sounds.

"So...?"

"I can't remember."

"Tell me."

"Nothing!"

"Tell me, Michael."

A special, unbelievably expensive present—a new bike. To commemorate the occasion. The Four Questions. He couldn't believe it. He couldn't wait to touch it. And just before the Seder he decided to slip away and take a ride. His own new bike. Gleaming black with chrome handbrakes and its own gearshift.

Now, like those men in their big limousines he could sail around the city—anywhere he chose. He took it to a friend's apartment to show it off. Unfamiliar with laws of bikes he left it outside when he went into the building. Only for a moment. When he returned with his friend it was gone. Vanished. How long had he known it—a few minutes? Had it ever really existed? It was as though the man's world—its mysterious workings, its oiling and bolting and clicking, the sensation of soaring powerfully over the sidewalk—was more than he deserved.

Reduced to his own feet again, sobbing, he ran all the way home thoughtlessly bursting into the apartment and shattering the festive mood. His father was outraged. Were his gifts— his rewards—of so little consequence? He pronounced the terrible punishment. No *yarmulke*, no Four Questions. His mother, a woman who squirmed around her husband for the slightest signs of recognition, pleaded briefly. Uselessly. Once committed, his father would not, could not, retreat. A sign of weakness for someone who took guidance in his everyday affairs from newspaper quotes of tough speeches made by the Israeli Prime Minister. A young cousin— a girl no less! (who later became a Hare Krishna)—was assigned to replace him.

By the time Michael had finished the story I was holding him to my breast, next to Reuven. Reuven's sucking sounded almost sorrowful.

"You're my man, Michael," I said.

Reuven's birth certificate. Next to religion, it said Christian. Michael looked at me suspiciously. (Oh, Michael, Michael, do you think I would be unfaithful so soon?")

"At the office they said we had to discuss it with a rabbi."

Michael insisted we call one right away.

How different from our sun-tanned rabbi in his Mexican shirt was this one who came wrapped in black, with neglected skin and teeth. What would he have thought of the man who married us with his guitar? Not much, it was clear. Michael told him how he had come to fight for Israel. The rabbi nodded with solemn politeness, but was interested in other questions. How had we met, how were we married, what kind of ceremony, what was my religious training, what about my parents, who was the baby's father? By the time the rabbi got around to the last question, he was not so polite.

"Who is the father?" Michael exploded.

Exactly, the rabbi responded. He, Michael, of the House of Cohen, more than anyone should have known. To marry an impure woman and try to pass her off as a Jew, her child as a Jew. Did he not realize that by Jewish law I was not in any way Jewish, therefore no child of our union would be Jewish? The ancient fathers had the wisdom to recognize the uncertainty of paternity in such circumstances. Perhaps if this woman—the rabbi barely glanced in my direction—made a serious effort to convert, studied under a real rabbi for a few years, made the required visits to the *mikvah* (the ritual bath)... but, of course, there would still be the matter of Reuven to consider. The rabbi excused himself. Fluttering blackness, he disappeared down the long row between the beds. After a silence, Michael began to mutter, softly at first: "*Dom*—Blood. *Sh'chin*—Boils. *Ts'fardaya*—Frogs. *Barad*—Hail. *Kinim*—Vermin."

"What are you saying, Michael."

"The ten plagues." His voice grew louder. "*Arbeh*—Locusts. *Arov*—Beasts. *Choshech*—Darkness. *Dever*—Cattle Disease. *Makat B'chorot*—Slaying of the First-Born."

"Michael..."

"*Rabbis!*"

By now Michael's voice was loud enough to be heard by the men in the other beds and their visitors. They turned toward us, saw the bandage on his head and turned back after brief pitying looks. Brain damage, they shrugged, what do you expect.

The night Michael was discharged from the hospital we came home and made love, again quietly, this time in order not to wake Reuven. It was as though we had to prove we were healed, were carrying on. There was a nervousness in our movements, each afraid that one would worry about the other, *spectatoring,* as they say. Michael so gentle, so cautious. Once I caught him rubbing his nose, took his hand and kissed it. As I ran my fingers through his hair I could feel the scar, the slight thickness of skin over the metal plate. From now on this would be the feeling of my lover, my Michael. I came, he came, we both laughed with relief and fell asleep.

In the middle of the night I found him sitting up. He couldn't face going back to the TV repair shop and fighting with his boss again. He wanted to go back home. Of course, I said sleepily. (*Of course!*) And I fell back to sleep dreaming of my champagne wedding and my black olive husband.

Well, easier said than done. We couldn't just pick up and leave, could we? Anyway, with Reuven we felt we should have something to go to, a job, some security. We wrote a few friends. I also dropped a note to Michael's parents telling them we were going back to the States. The friends wrote back: nothing definite, but we could stay with them while we looked. We also got a letter from Michael's mother. With ludicrously misspelled words, she recited their sorrows: his father was scheduled for cataract surgery; his legs had bad circulation, they were thinking he might need an operation on them as well; he wouldn't listen to the doctor who told him to stop smoking;

neighbors, after being burgled and mugged, were moving away—they had very few friends left; of the blacks who took their places she didn't want to say; the print shop which he had long ago sold—given away practically, since by the time he agreed to give it up, his computer-savvy competitors had already captured the Christmas card business—had been replaced by a record store which blasted such frightening music into the streets at all hours of the day and night. Would we at least join them for Passover Seder? Nothing definite, Michael, no jobs, I said. Should we go? To my surprise Michael said yes.

My sweet Michael. Nothing to prove anymore, I thought to myself, only this time I didn't say it.

When we took off from Lod, world-famous airport of Israel, I couldn't help smiling to myself as I looked down on the ramshackle buildings.

"Looks like Hollywood-Burbank," I said.

"I wish it was already," said Michael.

Michael's home was just as he had described it. The winding staircase, the dark echoes of a dilapidated Brooklyn tenement. I recognized his mother immediately. A small, timid woman, who after a moment's uncertainty, responded to my hug. I saw her bony hands trembling. The smells that surrounded her reminded me of my sycamore tree and orange blossoms: potato kugel, matzoh balls, chicken soup, sponge cake, honey cake. And her garden didn't hang from trees, but lay heaped on platters: great mounds of nuts and plums and oranges and bananas and raisins.

We passed the kitchen through the narrow hallway to the living room—and there amid the stuffed furniture, the glittering silver and glass stood the mahogany banquet table on its thick legs, there it presided. All exactly as Michael had described it. Except something was missing. And then I realized—we were almost the only ones there. The crowds, the buzzing excitement of Michael's stories were gone, replaced by a few odd people, one or two children, men in baggy business suits and their wives who stood around awkwardly and did not seem to know him.

And then I saw Michael's father. Did he look bitterly at his son, the one who tore apart his kingdom? As he awaited our approach his feeble hand rubbed his nose. Pale cheeks, moist lips, wispy hair, he sat, or rather was propped up by many pillows in a chair by the Seder table, there next to the candelabra and decanters, he held himself stiffly and presided. His greenish blue suit seemed to have been pasted on him, its smooth sheen concealing the wrinkles and lumpy joints that only his protruding neck and hands betrayed. Behind his thick glasses, his eyes, the same color as Michael's, were motionless, like two dead bees.

Michael hesitated, ignored the feeble outstretched hand and embraced him. The old man accepted the hug without moving, chin and jowls stiff and defiant. And yet, the old man's eyes never left Michael, even after he introduced me. Only when I put Reuven into his arms, then for the first time, did the old man smile. Reuven, naturally, went into a frightful howl. Behind me I heard a few whispers: "In the war...the first to reach the Suez."

"This is Christina. My wife," said Michael pointedly.

"You're late. We were waiting for you."

"We were held up in traffic," I explained.

"They were held up in traffic," Michael's mother repeated.

"What?"

"Traffic. They were held up in traffic."

"They should have taken the subway."

"He says you should have taken the subway."

"The subway doesn't go to the airport," Michael said.

"He says the subway doesn't go to the airport."

"He should have thought of that in the first place."

I started to apologize but Michael's father's eyes avoided me. "Everyone. Sit!" he commanded.

I took a chair next to a tense overweight woman who smiled briefly when I introduced myself; her eyes wandered curiously over my hair, then looked away. In an instant Reuven pulled at the tablecloth and knocked over her wine while her daughter, from the other side, began unwittingly to kick me under the table. I wondered: Do we breed our unconscious desires when we breed our children?

Meanwhile, as I tried to hold Reuven in one hand and clean up the wine with my napkin in the other, Michael's father had already begun the prayer. When I was done I leaned back and a thousand thoughts flooded my brain. The familiar chanting in Hebrew, the responsive readings, the wine ceremonies, the passing of herbs and *charosis*, the breaking of matzoh—all these sounds which commemorated the victory of Israel over Egypt, all these had private memories for me—lovers, places. I couldn't help smiling to myself. (How lucky I am, my memories are better than my fantasies.)

When did I first become aware of a harsher sound rasping beneath the soft chanting of the Seder? Like someone sawing, like something hissing, first here, then there. A young boy, wearing a crisp shirt and new tie, was reciting the Four Questions. I looked at Michael and saw how red and tense his face was. And then I looked around the room. The other men were staring at him angrily, but Michael kept his face buried in his Hagaddah. What was wrong?

And then I realized that Reuven was wearing a yarmulke. But Michael? His head was bare. He had put his yarmulke on Reuven. The whispers grew louder. Faces turned toward me resentfully. I started to reach for the cap on Reuven's head and felt my hand stopped by a fierce grip. It was Michael.

"Michael, what is it?"

Michael's father looked up. His eyes blinked around the room. Now he noticed something wrong.

"What is it?" he demanded.

Silence. Then one of the men spoke in Yiddish. A short growl. Everyone looked at Michael and me.

"Where is your yarmulke?" the old man demanded.

"On my head," said Michael quietly.

"Where? Show me!"

"Where you can't see it."

Another Yiddish growl and Michael's father saw the yarmulke on Reuven. "It's on the baby's head."

Again I started to take it off, but Michael looked at me, his eyes flaring. "Leave it!"

"Michael..."

"You stay out of this," his father shouted, looking at me for the first time.

Michael's voice rose to meet his. "She is my wife!"

"Your wife?"

"Apologize! Apologize to my wife!"

Michael's father turned to me once again and in his high-pitched quivering voice shouted at me while he shook his finger. "I...I... apologize? Like my son's yarmulke—I don't even see you!"

In a flash Michael crashed his fist down on his wine glass. Red wine splashed onto whiteness everywhere, shirts, blouses, the linen tablecloth, the wall, everywhere. (Michael, Michael, now I have to clean up after you, too.) Suddenly the room was in a turmoil, women shrieking, men rising in rage. In my arms Reuven shook and howled. With one last fierce look at me the old man fell back in his chair, sprawled amid the pillows, his chest heaving; his thick glasses slid down his face. Everyone rushed to help him and I burst into tears. A stroke, I thought. Only Michael's mother remained calm. She directed the men to carry him to their bedroom. I waited in my chair, shivering, holding Reuven tightly to me. Michael wanted to help but was kept away from the door. One by one the men came out of the bedroom scowling.

"How is he?"

"All right, all right," said Michael's mother. She obviously wanted to tell me something.

"Can I see him?" I asked.

The old woman shook her head. "I think it's better you should..."

Michael didn't wait for her to finish. He had already turned. "Let's go," he said.

We finished our dinner in the airport snack bar and flew on to California.

It was several months before Michael found the kind of job he was looking for, in a firm that made computer games. A hard time. Michael wasn't so patient anymore and we fought, over money, out of boredom, about Reuven, everything. We considered splitting. When things finally settled down I dropped a note to Michael's parents. The return letter had a new address on it. They had finally moved out of Flatbush to Long Island. Within days after they got there his father died. She had hoped we might make the funeral—hardly anyone did— but she didn't know where to reach us. On the other hand, if we had showed up who knows what would have happened? People fight about the silliest things. Wasn't that what made wars? And anytime you try to do something nice other things happen and before you know it you're doing everything wrong. Michael couldn't help smiling at her misspelled words (maybe he would remember to light a "yardsite" candle), but as he read the letter I saw him rub his nose and sink into a chair. When he was done he crumpled the letter up and threw it away.

Well, this war is over at last, I thought. He picked up a computer game, one his company made that he kept next to his chair, and started tapping on it. Reuven crawled over to him, looked up and started to pull himself up on his feet. Absently, Michael took him and put him in his lap. Right away Reuven grabbed for the computer game, but Michael snatched it away. And I caught myself smiling.

Michael, Michael. You won't miss the next one either.

Feldman, The Prophet

When Feldman rang the doorbell and
saw how the Websters stiffened at the
sound, pressing against each other as though
they preferred not to be seen with him, a familiar sour taste entered his mouth and he looked
away, reflexly appraising the house. Before he
got into adoptions Feldman had done real
estate. Once, you could pick up this kind of
single-story stucco, he remembered, built
during the war...Then another familiar sensation came rushing down on him, obliterating
his calculations, a miserable certainty only a
prophet could know: this deal was going to go
flat on its ass.

They could hear children shouting somewhere in the back. Woman probably owns it
outright. Community property settlement.
Like Sherrie, his ex. Although as soon as *that*
woman took over, she knocked the place down,
put up one of those lumber monsters with all

sorts of crazy windows and angles, gave each kid a separate room. Good old Sherrie. The first night they had spent together was in a jail full of migrant farm workers. The last in a Dr. Phil Marriage Boot Camp. Old Sherrie had really taken charge, as they say, just as Feldman had predicted. Although he hadn't predicted the details, such as how remorseless she would be.

Feldman rang again. He fingered his scalp and aimed a professional twitch of a smile at the Websters to relax them. They were standing there, faces screwed into simpering fright masks, a combination of forced grin and chewed lip. Denton Webster, loose moustache weighing down his bulky handsome face, Clare wide-eyed in purple-framed glasses—a pathetic parody now of the snazzy smiling photo they had put out with their brochure.

The door was yanked open, then immediately abandoned by someone who ran shouting into the house, "They're here! They're here!" Feldman pushed the door and gestured for the Websters to precede him. Once inside the two of them swelled up against the wall as though to advertise again, Well, yes, we're here, but we're not with that man over there.

And again Feldman looked away, this time to price the furnishings. For a moment his sensitive allergic nostrils balked, refused to take in air. Cheapness, like a stale aroma, rose from everything, from the worn blanket-covered couch, the laminated coffee table, the pebbly polyester stuffed chair, the ratty wicker chair, the clothes and toys and whatnot strewn about the room. Now, right now, Feldman thought, turning the sourness over with his tongue, at this very moment, his former law partners who had reorganized him out of the firm—during the annual retreat, in fact while he was rehearsing the wives' chorus line—were soaking in dark luxurious leather in spacious offices with panoramic views, discussing retirement and second careers. That too, he had seen coming, months ahead, but once again, not the details, such as how deftly his old friends would do it.

A semi-pretty woman in a faded plaid shirt hanging over corduroy jeans padded in from the kitchen with sticky hands held out as though they were palsied. Feldman tried to estimate how far along she was.

"Mrs. Garber?" said Feldman. Her bare feet matched the soiled beige of the carpet.

The woman nodded, trying to press a loose frizz of hair behind her ear with her wrist. "Hang on a sec," she said and backed into the kitchen. Two boys peeked out the door and squealed with a kind of glee that Feldman found unsettling.

"How we doing," said Feldman to the boys. He guessed they had been playing in the living room. A goldfish bowl sat on a patch of soggy carpet in one corner, surrounded by dozens of alkaline toy batteries. A solitary goldfish was looking at him warily. The woman returned wiping her hands with a towel.

"Mrs. Garber?" Feldman repeated. "Mr. and Mrs. Webster."

"How's it going," said Mrs. Garber.

"Denton and Clare," said Mr. Webster.

"Denton and Clare," the two boys giggled and fell on each other, punching.

"You guys want to go make yourself some chocolate?" said Mrs. Garber. The boys flung a brief defiant glance at Feldman, then slammed the kitchen door. Then came a racket of scraping chairs and banging cabinet doors.

"Quite a handful," Feldman smiled. The woman scowled as though he had just muttered something of questionable sanity. "No school today?" Feldman added, stretching the smile, calculating the necessity for a little more small talk.

"'Disruptive'," they said. "I told 'em I'd be *disruptive* too if I had to sit all day listening to those sicko teachers."

Feldman started to nod affably, but an involuntary intake of breath and a stinging in his nostrils cut it short.

"Well," he said, flapping his hands. "Can we sit down? My clients have a few questions. And you have questions too, Mrs. Garber, I'm sure."

They pulled two chairs—the stuffed chair and the wicker chair—toward the couch to make a sort of circle. Meanwhile the racket from the kitchen continued. Every moment Feldman expected a horrible climactic crash, something—or someone—hitting the floor. But the woman behaved as though the noises were nothing more than ordinary city sounds.

"Well," said Feldman, preparing to sit in the wicker chair (it seemed the cleanest); then observing the broken struts of straw ready to impale his suit, he pushed sideways to the couch. This left the wicker chair to Mrs. Webster, who was too nervous to notice its condition.

"Well," said Feldman again as they sat, and as he looked around he felt the sensation again, a seeping unutterable depression, as though the sourness would spill out of his fixed smile if he were not careful. What was it? The inevitable decaying of ancestral powers? A blurring of vision—that peculiar blindness of prophets, which obscured the path ahead while lighting perimeters others could not see?

This whole deal thing was headed for disaster. He knew from the moment he stood in front of the house. Before he even saw the woman, when he saw the Websters with their screwed-on faces, saw the house, heard the screams of the children.

They were waiting for him to begin.

"Well," Feldman nodded to Mrs. Webster, "Why don't you go first."

Mrs. Webster unclenched her fist and revealed a tightly folded sheet of paper, which she spread shakily on her lap. "First of all," she said as though from a prepared speech, "I'm happy to see you don't smoke."

"Ha! Two, three packs a day, if you really want to know," Mrs. Garber exclaimed, which made Mrs. Webster start. "Quit," she added, "when I got double walking pneumonia," which made Mrs. Webster smile and place a little check mark on the paper. She went on to the next category.

"Alcohol? Medicine...I mean, you know, *drugs*?" The very idea that such items tainted the world seemed to fluster her. She looked to Feldman for help. Feldman helped by tilting his head toward Mrs. Garber, indicating thereby that a frank answer would be tolerated.

"Beer now and then. Three. Four. I'm no alcoholic, if that's what you mean." A hint of irritation rasped her voice. "How about aspirin? Aspirin okay?"

"She means, you know... *drugs*," said Feldman, but he too was becoming irritated. Mrs. Webster's questions were nibbling at the edges, would take forever. Without waiting for an answer, Feldman took over. "Perhaps you wouldn't mind telling us," he said, "how you arrived at the nine thousand figure."

Just then the two boys peered out from the kitchen. They were holding glasses of chocolate milk, their faces draining copious chocolate beards. When Feldman caught their eye they both spurted mouthfuls of milk in his direction, then squealed and slammed the door.

The Websters exchanged glances and chuckled audibly so the woman would not feel embarrassed. "Hey, hey, you two," said Mrs. Garber mildly, but when she looked at Feldman it was as though she had found worms on his face. "If it's too much, you shouldn't be wasting my time."

The Websters fluttered, darted looks of panic at Feldman.

"No, no, of course not," said Feldman quickly. "Just inquiring." His voice took on a little more control, soothed. "For legal purposes." He noticed the two boys peeking out from the kitchen again. His glance connected him to the taller of the two.

"Know what?" said the boy.

"What's that?" said Feldman.

"Back in the kitchen, okay?" said Mrs. Garber.

"My mother's pregnant."

"She's pregnant," chimed in the smaller boy. "You know what that means?"

"Okay, back in the kitchen, okay?" said Mrs. Garber.

The two boys giggled and slammed the kitchen door.

"Watch the milk," Mrs. Garber sang after them, then looked back at Feldman, her expression once again distastefully curious. She waited.

"My clients were wondering how you arrived at the figure."

"What difference does it make?"

"If it's for expenses..."

"I just picked a number. A thousand a month."

"You can claim costs..."

"It's what I want."

"Otherwise there's a legal problem."

"It's what I want," Mrs. Garber repeated stubbornly.

Feldman became aware that the Websters had picked up Mrs. Garber's expression, were looking at him with the same distaste. So *this* was how he spent his day. *This* was his life's work, *this* his sweatshop world. It was the look his partners had given him when Feldman announced he was tired of mergers and venture financing and wanted to do more "human services." Feldman hadn't intended any quotation marks, but they were there in the letter of termination.

Feldman felt his nostrils starting to burn, pulled out his handkerchief, dabbed and looked. He was subject to nosebleeds. Mrs. Webster consulted her piece of paper.

"Does your job expose you to any toxic chemicals," she asked, pencil poised.

"Whatever that means. No," said Mrs. Garber.

"What kind of things do you do," said Mr. Webster with practiced affability.

"When I get work, you mean?"

"What do you plan to do with the money, Mrs. Garber," Feldman interrupted, without even a glance at the Websters. All he wanted now was to get this over as soon as possible, to get out of the house. No blood yet, but the burning had moved up into his head. A body sign. And the woman's bare feet gave him another. Lacking details, he knew this much: it was spinning straight down. Trailing smoke. Time to jump.

"Go into business," said Mrs. Garber, squirming her toes.

"With nine thousand dollars? What kind of business?"

"Would you tell us about the father," said Mrs. Webster. "Could you say a word about him physically and...spiritually?"

Feldman made sure he didn't lose eye contact. "What if you don't get the money? Will you keep the baby or give it away?"

"Keep it, of course. Why should I give it away?"

"If you wouldn't give it away, how do we know you wouldn't want it back?"

"If I sell it to you...'

"You can't sell it, Mrs. Garber. That's illegal."

"You were going to tell us about the father," Mrs. Webster encouraged.

"You see, Mrs. Garber. My clients have to feel confident that you'll never want it back no matter how much they pay you. Otherwise..." Feldman pinned her with his look, then shrugged, archly, deliberately, in the time-honored tradition, sure that the Websters would be grateful for his shrewdness. But Mrs. Webster pushed past him, her voice cracking.

"Can you give us some kind of picture?"

Mr. Webster shifted and coughed, occupied the pause with his admonitory rumble. Feldman glanced down and saw blood bloom in his handkerchief as Mrs. Garber, released, burst free. Yes. A wonderful man. Dark-haired, good-looking, very good-looking, a businessman, but sweet and, yes, spiritual. She, you know, dated him a few times, and one of those times...

The blood kept coming. Feldman excused himself, asking directions to the bathroom. Enrapt, the Websters seemed no longer aware of him.

Once inside the small room, humid with damp towels, Feldman turned on the cold water and searched in the medicine cabinet for cotton. The shelves were crowded with jars and bottles, powders and ointments, creams and little black brushes, Q-tips yellowed with earwax—the woman apparently re-used them—but no cotton. Among other intimacies, Feldman learned that the woman employed mint-flavored dental floss, Ampicillin for urinary tract infections, and the same health chain moisturizer his ex-wife used.

Now the blood was dripping relentlessly and Feldman had to keep his head bent over the sink to avoid spattering everywhere. He soaked his handkerchief and pressed the cold wet mass against his face. Experience had taught him to plug his bleeding nostril as soon as possible, he'd have to use toilet paper, but when he looked over at the toiled bowl and saw the unflushed turds he nearly reeled. A children's bathroom—he had forgotten what it was like. The stench tore at his nostrils, more than that, it leaped at him—the act of defilement. It was as though the hatred of the two small boys—sparked the moment they saw him—had ambushed him in here.

There was a knock at the door. "Just a minute," said Feldman soggily through the handkerchief. When he opened the door, Mrs. Webster was standing there, eyes a shiny film behind her glasses.

"You've gone and made her mad at us," she protested.

"Excuse me, Mrs. Webster," said Feldman through his wet handkerchief.

"If you only knew..."

"Come," said Feldman, drew her into the bathroom and shut the door. Once inside, Mrs. Webster broke down and sobbed.

"If you only knew..."

Feldman sat her on the toilet seat and out of respect flushed the toilet. "Believe me, Mrs. Webster, I know," said Feldman, and in his voice he heard the same skillful, mournful resonance of Zweifach, his lawyer, when that man told him, actually had put his hand on his shoulder while telling him, his wife's terms. "She's nothing but trouble, this woman, believe me," said Feldman, placing his hand on her shoulder.

But Mrs. Webster did not believe. Indeed, the look on her face as she stiffened was one of total sneering disbelief. Feldman felt his hand float off her shoulder. She was glaring at him.

"Now and then," Feldman confessed, "I get nosebleeds." And as soon as he said it he knew that he had exposed the corrupt secret of his soul to this woman who up to now had only strongly suspected it. Mrs. Webster emitted a loud sob and shook her head. Feldman could see he was another knot in the long string of her misfortunes.

"Look, Mrs. Webster. I would be so happy for you to take it away. Take away the other two. In my opinion, in this woman's hands, they're going to grow up to be criminals."

"You made her *mad*."

"Made her *mad?* That woman? Mrs. Webster, all her life that woman's been mad. Excuse me for being so blunt. That woman, I'll tell you what she's going to do. That woman will take your money, plunk it in some business she knows nothing about, she'll buy on credit, pile up bills, raise the hopes of a few people who desperately need jobs, then go broke. Then she'll sue to get the baby back. Believe me, I know. I can see it coming. Like it's right here in front of me. Mrs. Webster, I don't get fooled anymore. Such people, they make as much pain as they can. Excuse me, can I have the seat? I got to put my head back."

Just then the doorknob rattled. A pounding on the door was followed by muffled giggles. They heard the two boys running away, squealing, "They're *both* in there. They're *both* in there."

Mrs. Webster got the door open just in time to face her husband who appeared to be somewhat out of breath. "What's going on," said Mr. Webster, his moustache disheveled.

"Nothing, nothing," Feldman reassured him, leaning back. "We're in chambers, as they say." Surely the joke, if not the sight of this funny little lawyer in his dignified suit, stretched out on a toilet, squashing his face with a wet bloody handkerchief, would lighten the occasion, Feldman thought, but he was wrong.

"Now he has a nosebleed," said Mrs. Webster.

Mrs. Garber appeared.

"I could use some cotton, Mrs. Garber," said Feldman. But Mrs. Garber had none. She tilted her head, peered.

"Hang on a sec."

"When you said nine thousand dollars," said Mr. Webster, "I assumed it was inclusive."

"Plus expenses, plus expenses, I said," said Mrs. Garber into the cabinet under the sink.

There was a commotion at the door as the two boys pushed to see what was going on. They leered at Feldman with chocolate-smeared faces. Feldman saw they were clutching handfuls of small batteries. He turned away and closed his eyes.

"There seem to be difficulties," said Mr. Webster.

"Mr. Feldman!"

Feldman opened his eyes, saw Mr. Webster glaring at him and closed them again.

Just then Mrs. Garber uttered the kind of cry one makes on hearing a raunchy joke. Feldman heard a tearing of paper. "Here we go," said Mrs. Garber. Feldman saw Mrs. Garber holding a cylinder of what appeared to be white cotton under his nose. She pulled away the bloody handkerchief and Feldman felt a surge of pain as she pushed the tampon deftly and decisively into his nostril.

They waited.

Feldman stood up carefully and looked in the mirror. The string was still dangling from the other end of the protruding tampon, but Feldman didn't dare touch it for fear of unleashing the blood.

"That's got the sucker," said Mrs. Garber.

Feldman gingerly straightened his suit, looked around without speaking, then cautiously stepped into the living room. The sight of the circle of chairs, the ratty wicker chair, his place on the couch waiting for him, sent the sourness in his mouth bursting into his head. He steadied himself, waited. Had the bleeding started again? No. But he couldn't go on, that was certain.

Just then a loud clang came from the corner where the fishbowl sat, followed by a shriek of glee from the other corner of the living room. The goldfish swished, then poised quiveringly. At first Feldman couldn't make out what had happened. Then he saw the taller of the two boys take aim and fling something at the fishbowl. One of the batteries. It clanged against the glass, and again the fish swirled frantically, then froze, its gills panting.

When the two boys caught sight of Feldman they of course shrieked with laughter. But Feldman, ignored them, turned his back on them and looked at the Websters and Mrs. Garber. The string flicked under his nose, which reminded him he should thank Mrs. Garber for helping him. Instead he heard himself addressing her with great dignity.

"For all I know, Mrs. Garber," Feldman heard himself say "You have it in mind to sell this baby, then grow another baby and sell that one, too. And another one and another one. Why not? That's just the way your mind runs."

Mr. and Mrs. Webster were squinting at him furiously.

"The baby. The goldfish. You know what's going to happen?"

There was another clang from the fishbowl and again a shout from the other corner of the living room.

Mr. Webster screwed his handsome bulky face into a smile.

"Goodbye, Mr. Feldman," he said, offering his hand.

Feldman shook his head, flicking the string back and forth. "You people," he said hoarsely, the phrase ripping out of him like flesh, vengefully, out of his flesh, out of his soul. "You people will destroy everything."

"Goodbye, Mr. Feldman."

Feldman left the house, taking one step at a time, carefully. At the bottom of the steps, he looked around, finished his appraisal. This he knew, this he could predict—someday, someone would come along, tear this place down too, put up one of those lumber monsters with huge windows, crazy angles. Make himself a terrific deal. Only it wouldn't be Feldman. This, too, he knew. He walked to his car, tampon still sticking out of his nose, string still dangling. But he didn't touch it. He knew what would happen if he did. For Feldman now, as always, the fear of bleeding was greater than the pain of humiliation. But nothing, nothing was worse than the certainty of knowing.

Feldman drove away. Proudly, prophetically.

The Appointment

Look, I'll show you the card. Jorge Gonzales. YOU HAVE AN APPOINTMENT. See? All these months I keep it for him in the drawer with my kerchiefs, the rosary, all my clinic cards. Every day I take it out and look at the calendar. Never, not once, do I miss an appointment for my children. Look how it's smeared with rouge. Smell the perfume.

Serafina, she grunts when I show it to her. Like this she turns it over, then pushes it back at me. "*Esta loca,*" she says.

"Speak English," I say to her.

Serafina looks at me like she tastes something sour.

"I'm not crazy," I say to her. "It's an appointment. I have to go." What else can I tell her? I *keep* my appointments. That's what I can tell her. Not like you, and all the rest of you.

So what does she do? In her slippers she goes and sits in front of the television. But I can tell she is watching me out of the corner of her eye.

See? Look at this. I bring Jorge's shoes, a pair of socks, a shirt, shorts. Everything washed and ironed. These same clothes he wears in the picture over the sewing machine. In the picture, Francisco, my husband, stands next to me. Serafina, she is his aunt, she sits in front. Jorge is with Graciela and Julieta on the donkey. The poor little animal is painted to look like a zebra. Francisco makes a deal with the man.

It rains. The man has no business. Francisco has money for putting new seat covers on an Anglo sailor's car. In a bar they make the deal. Francisco runs home. Quick, he says. I pick some flowers for the girls—real flowers, not those paper things they sell in the streets. All dressed up like we're going to see the Pope. We squeeze around the painted donkey and the man takes our picture. The whole family, the same price he charges one Anglo tourist.

In the picture, Francisco looks nervous. Why? I don't know why. Maybe he is afraid the man will change his mind and charge him a whole lot of money. But his face, it reminds me when Jorge was born. When Francisco stands in the door of my hospital room he acts strange. Like a stranger. Why, I thought. Is it because of me? In the mirror I see my face. *Mi madre!* How bad I look. Francisco and another man from the shop. They are standing in the doorway. Afraid to come in. Francisco smiling, but so nervous. Like he brings his friend along to help him. Eight children, I want to tell him, and you're still shy about women's things, Francisco?

Jorge was not easy. He takes a long time. The doctors examine me. After they finish the nurse snaps the curtain back and shouts, "Not yet. Little more. Understand? *Un poco mas!*"

"I understand," I tell them in English.

But, at last it's over. How happy I am. "You like him?" I ask.

But Francisco just stands there in the doorway. The doctors say something is wrong with Jorge. *What?* Something with his heart, but they can fix it. *Gracias a Dios!* What miracles the Anglo doctors can do.

An operation. It makes Francisco nervous. The doctors say Jorge might die. Serafina is angry. That's what I get for going to *la clinica*. She hates this place. Once, a specialist does not see her. The other doctors, they squeeze her breasts and belly with their silky hands. But do they give her the shot she needs? No. They say to her, "Lose weight." Take Jorge to the *curandero*, she keeps telling me, but I tell her No!

One morning I find a bowl of water with egg and pieces of palm under Jorge's bed. From then on I watch very closely. I must protect Jorge from her and her old fashioned ways.

"Can the *curandero* fix the holes in Jorge's heart?" I say to her. "Can he do such miracles?"

But the old woman says nothing. When I'm not looking she tries to sneak on suction cups. When I catch her she spits on the floor.

"Stop spitting," I shout at her, and Jorge starts to cry.

"*Esta loca,*" she tells everyone. It is *mal de ojo,* the Evil Eye. If I want Jorge to live, if I want miracles, I must let her take him to the *curandero.*

Meanwhile, the doctors say Jorge is not ready for the miracle. He doesn't like to eat. He learns to walk, but he is small, smaller even than Graciela. The doctors say he must grow a little bigger before they can fix his heart. "Just a little more," they say. "*Un poco mas.*"

Francisco says do not listen to Serafina. Anglo doctors, they are the best in the world. Every day you read such amazing things. Every day on television a new miracle.

But it is not a good thing to make Serafina mad. Years ago she married an Anglo. So she has a Social Security card. Now, her friends, they use her number, and if money comes Serafina is very honest. She finds them and gives it to them. Everyone trusts Serafina. She can make a lot of trouble.

So today, I say to her, "Serafina, I have to get dressed." Just Serafina and me in the bedroom. If Francisco was home, she would get up, aah, naah, and leave the room. She knows I want to be alone. But what does she do? She pretends she cannot hear me. She keeps her ear cupped like this to the television. Outside the children are playing. The women are in the kitchen talking to Dolores, my oldest daughter. Always the old woman likes to hear gossip. But you think this time? No. I must get dressed while Serafina watches me. For her, everything I put on tells her something. This old woman, she always forgets things, she always asks: Where are my slippers, where are my teeth, but she remembers all my clothes. Everything. She knows where I get my slips, my bras, my stockings, my panties, my dresses. She remembers every time I wear them. I put on my clothes, she is checking on me.

"*Esta loca.*" That's what she always tells Francisco.

Crazy. This old woman calls me crazy. For what? Because I speak English? So I can get a good job someday? Citizenship even? Like my children? All my babies I am very careful to have across the border.

And *especially* I keep my appointments. For checkups. For shots and examinations. So all my children when they start looking for jobs, they will be as strong and healthy like Anglo children.

So what do I do? I turn my back on Serafina and pick out my best bra, the yellow lace one from my wedding. Then I worry the bra is too fancy. Serafina will tell Francisco I am carrying on with one of the Anglo doctors, so next I put on old cotton panties I share with Dolores and Alissandre. And my oldest slip. I pull a few loose strings before I put it on. And then I get real mad at myself. Look how I'm dressing! To suit Serafina's big nose. Right away I pull down this, my purple dress. It shows my knees. Right away I worry. Who wears such a silly dress to the clinic? The doctors and nurses will look at me and their eyes will say, "Another one." The woman at the desk will ask to see my card and make me wait while they check the machine to see if I have any unpaid bills.

But too late. Serafina will tell Francisco... *Francisco?*...the whole barrio, if I try on dresses just to go to *la clínica*. She will hiss to everyone, "Modesta is carrying on with one of the doctors."

Then I look at my watch. I have to hurry. I check my purse to make sure I have enough money. Sometimes my children steal from me. If I'm on a bus or in a store I see my money is gone I want to shout out loud, so everyone will hear what my children do to me. But instead I cry. Why should my children have to steal? But then I think something else. Isn't it better they steal from me than from a stranger who will put them in jail?

I look at Serafina. Serafina shakes her head. "*El doctor no esta alla.*"

"The doctor is there," I say. "See. I have an appointment."

But she shakes her head and doesn't look.

It's true, though, what she says. Sometimes, many times, the doctor is not here. Once, Serafina gets all dressed up to come here. To see an important specialist. She even borrows money to take a taxi across the border. But when she shows up they say the doctor is not here. He is in another city giving a speech. The woman at the desk says, "Old woman, why are you so mad? The doctor will be happy to see you another day." But Serafina is really mad. The woman at the desk makes it sound like one day is as good another. After all what does this old woman do all day but sit around? She is Mexican herself, the woman at the desk. You think that makes Serafina feel better? Right there, in front of the whole waiting room she shouts and spits on the floor. Never, she says, *never* is she coming back to *la clinica!*

Now, who do you think is *loca?*

Still, I think, maybe she's right. So many women, they come all the way here and the woman says, "Go home, come back another time." Even though they have an appointment. Imagine. You wait for such a long time at the border. The guard with his dark glasses looks through your purse. Looks at your clothes. You show him the clinic card. You wait for the bus.

And when you get here they tell you it's a mistake. The doctor you are supposed to see is not here. Someone writes the wrong date on the card. Or the wrong time, so you arrive too late.

Or, to tell the truth, sometimes the women lose their cards. You see, me, I am so careful where I keep mine. They go on a day they think is the right one, only it isn't. Other specialists are here. The woman at the desk smiles and looks down her nose. Your disease is not so big as the diseases we see today.

Today the bus is crowded. Mothers with children, old people with canes, young people with casts and crutches. Everyone grunting and limping, everyone laughing and joking, you know? Going to *la clinica?* they say. A hot day for it. *Si.* A hot day for it. I sit and look at the children until they catch my eye and I turn away.

So many children, I think. Me, I have eight. Eight children. Would you believe it? Now I know it's too many. My mother, she had thirteen. Five are still living. I think so. Two brothers, who knows? They have trouble in Guadalajara and have to hide. Some men say they owe them money. My mother, she cries for weeks. There is talk of shooting. Every day my poor mother is sad or scared. Some people say bad luck comes like rain, so protect yourself with many children. But I ask you, is thirteen children enough? And how does it protect you? Now I know the truth. The more children, the more bad luck.

I think about this a lot when I am carrying Jorge. I tell Francisco we must stop. At first he cannot understand what I mean. Stop...being man and woman in bed? He cannot say the word. No, I say to him. We must do what the Anglo does, have our nights in bed, but stop making children. Francisco tells me he hears of this, too. But how does one do such things? He is too embarrassed to ask anybody. Go ask the priest, he tells me. Not a Mexican priest, but an Anglo. This priest says I must ask the doctor for something. At first Francisco does not believe me. The priest says this? Ask him yourself, I tell him.

Francisco goes. He comes back shaking. Men can have an operation on their private parts. The priest says it will take only a few minutes. Another miracle. But I see Francisco doesn't like the idea. He shakes as he tells me this. What else does he say? The priest also says the doctor can do something to me.

And so, Jorge is our last child. When he is born I have the operation. You can see why I am worried when Francisco looks at me strangely. Am I no longer a woman to him, I think.

But later, when I learn about Jorge, and I remember how much pain he gave me, I think something else. Is God punishing me? Is the priest *un brujo*?

But how can that be? Isn't Jorge a beautiful baby? And don't the doctors say they can fix him? Can *un brujo* make such miracles? And as for Francisco, he loves me just as much as ever in the bed. He is a good husband, even if he does not try so hard to learn English. He always brings us clothes and gives me money for food. And he does not drink any more than the other men, maybe a little bit less, because he always comes home at night and comes into bed to sleep with me.

I remember when I first get married, the smell of his sweat, the smell of a man's sweat so close to me. And the smell of beer coming out of his mouth and nose at night, all this is difficult for me. When I was a girl, the house I live in is in the country. I sleep only with my sisters, never with my father or my older brothers. I tell you this, because I know the kind of things people say about us who come from the country.

And Jorge. Even if he is not healthy, even if he is sick, he is special. My last child. I will never have another. It is like knowing that someone is about to die. You think about that person very hard, you want to feel the person next to you all the time. Sometime I am cooking in the kitchen and all the children are laughing and shouting, but only I hear Jorge. I stop and listen.

You think I do not love my other children just as much? You're wrong. Carlos, Dolores,

Alissandre, Ernesto, Graciela, Humberto, Julieta. Do I not talk about them as much? I love them just as much. It is just that...what is it? It is like a whole lot of people making music, you know what I mean, people singing, all of them making beautiful music. But now it is Jorge's time to sing out. It is his voice I hear most.

You think it is any different for the others? All my children, all of them, dig in the dirt and play with the hose. All of them get covered with mud. But it is only Jorge's face I see right now, covered with mud. His whole body covered with mud, his clothes, his shoes, a mess. And now I cry when I think how angry I get at him for getting dirty. For what? For dirt? They say Anglos throw away their clothes when they get dirty. Throw away their cars. Even their children, they say. Should I be like them? Is this why I want to learn English, so I can be like them? Then as I look out the bus window I think to myself, You sound old, Modesta. Like Serafina. You are getting old.

When the bus stops at the hospital and everyone gets out, I follow the green line. I show the woman at the desk the appointment card and she looks in the book.

"Gonzales," she says. She puts a little check.

I sit down. So, there is no mistake. The appointment is today, now, and the doctor is here. What a good feeling to be in *la clinica*, in this place of miracles. I see the doctors and nurses working. So clean, so healthy. And I remember Francisco, how nervous he is in this place. How shy he is to talk about personal things.

Here, I can talk about anything. Personal things, anything. I can show the doctors any part of my body, show them ugly things I am afraid to look at myself, and they never make faces.

True, they are cold, the doctors and nurses, they are cold. But what do I care if the world of miracles is a cold place.

But, you know I feel a sadness deep inside me, like water at the bottom of a well. Such a long time is that sadness inside me.

Then I hear the nurse: "Gonzales!" I follow her. She does not look at me any special way as she closes the door, but I think why does she look at me that way?

I wait a long time.

Outside the door I hear whispering. The door opens and in come two doctors. A woman doctor and you. The woman doctor, she wears a white coat and her name. But who are you, I think. You also wear your name but no white coat. You do not look at me like other doctors. You look only into my eyes.

"Mrs. Gonzales?" the woman doctor says.

"Yes."

"*Aqui esta el doctor ...*"

"I speak English," I say to her.

"Oh. This is Dr. Hernandez. He's a Psychiatrist."

"Yes?"

"He's here to help you."

Then I see that you are both looking at Jorge's clothes. I see how tightly I am holding them.

"He will make you better," she says.

"I see," I say to her. And she goes out. And I look at you. And I think—maybe this will be the miracle.

Teaching Rounds

This morning on rounds I learn that a patient has died because of a mistake made by the ward team during the night. They are visibly upset when they tell me this. I am sad about the patient, of course, a young man with AIDS, but I am even more concerned about the impact of this mistake on the doctors I am teaching, young residents and their acolyte students. The patient was about to die in any case, whereas my trainees have their whole professional life ahead of them. Medicine is a terrible taskmaster, imposing an unrealistic standard of perfection. I try to soften the blow by regaling them with one of my many aphorisms: *"If it's true you learn from your mistakes, someday I will know everything."*

I like the sound of my voice when I say this. It conveys a combination of dignity and humility, appropriate for an attending physician who wants to command respect and at the same time bridge the gap to the young. We sit in the doctor's office, surrounded by medical records, they in their scruffy, slept-in whites, I in my long white masterly coat. Their eyes are wide with appreciation. These are teaching rounds. I regard them as a sacred time and, following a tradition I inherited from my own great teachers of the past, I instruct the ward clerk and nurses to interrupt us only for the most dire emergencies.

During these sessions I often make use of stories from my own life as a doctor-in-training. Once dismissed as mere anecdotes, such stories are now called Narratives and are highly regarded in academic centers as important teaching techniques. Today, I draw from my file of stories: Mistakes I Made Back When I Was in Your Shoes. A woman with cancer who died a terrible death from intestinal obstruction because I neglected to pay attention to her bowels while treating her pain with large doses of morphine. A young woman with urinary tract infection who died suddenly of gram-negative sepsis while I dithered over which antibiotic to give her. I learned from these mistakes, I tell them. Now I know better. Always check the bowels when you're giving morphine, and never dither when there's a possibility of gram-negative sepsis. This morning I tell them about another patient, a young man named Ramon Romita.

I was an intern when I first saw Ramon one Sunday morning in Emergency. For some reason he could not get over the "flu." Tough, cocky, captain of his high school basketball team, Ramon planned to make use of the summer to perfect his skills while working for Park and Recreation. He was hoping, his family was hoping, everyone in his high school was hoping he would come back senior year and lead his team to a championship. But early in July he began to have trouble keeping up with his buddies. He had lost his speed, his moves, his strength, his endurance. When he lost his jump shot he agreed to see a doctor.

The neighborhood doctor he consulted gave him a shot of penicillin and sent him on his way. When that didn't work the doctor went through his cabinet of free samples to no avail. By the time I saw him a week or so later in Emergency he could barely climb onto the examining table. I was less than a month into my training, but after noting his fever and rapid pulse on his ER sheet and observing his pasty, bloodless flesh, his shambling struggles, and after feeling the lump of spleen, I already had a good idea of what was going on. His mother and father followed every move I made with frightened scowls. Something was terribly wrong, and they were right. Their son had acute leukemia.

Right away I played God. For starters I used the word, leukemia, without collapsing. They, being mere mortals, surely would have collapsed if I had not already sat them down. Then, in a voice I knew was as awesome as it was calm I explained to them what was happening, why Ramon was weak and tired (his oxygen-carrying red cells had dropped to about a third of normal), why he had fever (there were so many leukemic white cells they were heating his body up like a crowded bus). I answered their flailing questions with precise words that staked down their wind-blown fears. I spoke of miracles. We had drugs, powerful drugs that could fight off the disease, chase it away. Right there in front of them I put in a page for Hematology-Oncology. I told the Romitas I would see to everything.

From that day forth the whole family locked in on me as their miracle worker. *El Salvador.* And even though Ramon's chemotherapy was being directed by Heme-Onc the family agreed to nothing, no change in medications, no alteration of dose, no blood test, no X-ray without first checking with me. We had *bonded,* as the fashionable phrase goes. All the other doctors and nurses knew this and accepted it—happily, for it freed them from the tedium of donning sterile cap, gown, mask and gloves every time a blood culture had to be drawn or a festering rectum probed or a transfusion line unplugged. Most of all it freed them from having to answer the hundreds of daily questions and complaints.

Even though I was only an intern amidst battalions of celebrated specialists, no less than *El Salvador* was I, the one who first reached out his hand, touched their son's wilting body, spoke the words and raised him. *El Salvador.* Even though the terrible stuff I caused to be dripped into his veins made him sick as hell for weeks. For it seemed not only to serve as further proof of my powers, but also to satisfy a deep sense of Manichean drama, that the purging of evil required such dreadful cataclysms.

But Ramon, as it turned out, was on the wrong side of the percentages. He had the most ruthless form of leukemia. And although I always couched my daily reports in what I thought was realistic optimism, I was no fool: it was the optimism everyone heard, not the realism. We were all joined in an unspoken conspiracy against fate. Didn't I tell them miracles were possible? Ramon was going to beat the odds, now, during basketball season, and ever after.

And Ramon did get better. He even returned to Park and Recreation before the summer was over and resumed playing basketball. No one expected him right away to be as sharp as he was before he got sick, so every successful jump shot, every stolen pass, every rebound that fell into his hands served as confirming signs from heaven. Rare, yes, but how often do *you* receive signs from heaven?

The first relapse occurred just after school had started. Because we were following his blood counts closely we could tell when things were going sour even before Ramon could. Despite the minor rebellion in the outlying provinces of the blood, he, Ramon, safe in the central capital was getting stronger, taller, handsomer every day. A sheen of black hair, a downy hint of Don Juan moustache. His parents could not contain their gratitude, and the aunts and uncles and sisters and cousins who surrounded him in their shimmery dresses and shirts and plied me with Mexican pastries were like celebrants at Lourdes or Fatima.

And once again the magic worked. We treated the relapse with another batch of witches brew and within a month I could tell the Romita's that the leukemic white cells had been chased away. If the Romita's were believers before, now they were idolaters. My sessions with the Romita faithful could have been painted on the ceiling of the Sistine Chapel.

Did I actually believe this nonsense myself? I'm afraid I did. I was trapped in it as much as they were. I had already become this young basketball star. Were not the two of us—prancy and snazzy as we were—put on earth to live? Old geezers in other rooms were finishing their tour, but surely not young studs like us. It made no sense. Especially when every week or so another best-seller came out declaring that all you had to do was *think positively*, make those silly little cancer cells laugh and roll helplessly on the floor while you *took charge of your life!* Maybe—no not maybe—*Yes* there would be a miracle, *yes* he would survive. *Yes* I would be forgiven for allowing this bloated reverence for life and this obscene reverence for me to go unchecked.

Then came the final relapse, the most terrible day of reckoning. Ramon showed up again in Emergency, looking worse than ever, more pasty and shambling, his hair sopping wet with fever, his heart thrashing almost audibly in the room, his spleen this time so engorged it could be seen bulging out of his belly. I arranged to have him admitted.

The Romita's all chipped in to pay for a private room and packed it with a fiesta day crowd—faces shiny with expectation, primped for the occasion in holiday suits and color-ful dreses—awaiting the arrival of *El Salvador* and his next miracle. They landscaped the room with sweet-smelling flowers and dazzling paper imitations. They brought in extra chairs, crowded along the windowsill, pressed around his bed, squeezed his hands, rubbed his feet. When I arrived, all sound ceased, a path parted for me, and I entered bearing my talismans, an IV tray and two units of blood.

And there, before the throng of worship-pers, I failed. By then, my reputation for locating a delicate vein amid Ramon's fibrous tangles had become legendary. *El Salvador,* unlike those clumsy lab techs, gave one swift stroke and was in, followed customarily by a chorus of sighs and Ramon's assertion that he didn't feel a thing. A small deed, true, but one of heroic proportions to ordinary mortals who faint at scratches.

But this time my suave thrust came up dry. I prodded about with my finger. The needle seemed to be in the right place. But it was

unaccountably insubordinate. Perhaps a minute plane of tissue separated it from the vein.
I pushed, causing a small outcry. I wiggled,
tugged at the skin, nothing. Nothing except
pain, and more pain, which made me cringe
along with Ramon, as though the needle were
clawing inside *me*. Meanwhile I could feel my
fingers grow cold and lose their safe-cracker's
touch. I became aware of a silence consolidat-
ing behind my back, a dreadful silence, a dark
doom that mocked the Romita's festive prepa-
rations. (Would they ever again wear those
shimmery shirts and dresses, those flowery ties,
without remembering?) For the first time they
saw the battle turning against them, their god
sprawled before the gods of their enemy.

Again and again I failed—meanwhile
never willing to admit defeat, never calling for
help—while Ramon, who finally could take
it no longer, unleashed an endless torrent of
curses. The Romitas saw their god abject and
helpless. And so I was. With me still yanking
the needle back and forth under Ramon's
howls, he died, cringing and squirming. To my
shame, it never occurred to me, *El Salvador*, to
show mercy, give him morphine and let him
stretch out and pass away in peace.

"And so you see," I tell my ward team, shaking my head ruefully, bringing my cautionary

tale to its conclusion, "the most lasting lessons come from our mistakes. Ramon taught me the lesson of pride. If it's true you learn from your mistakes, someday I'll know everything."

I have told that story many times to many doctors-in-training. But this time as I look around the silent room I note something odd in those wide eyes, eyes that I thought had been gazing at me appreciatively, admiringly. Is there a glint of ironic amusement? Even something harder—a bloodshot, weary anger? They know I do not like it when they are sloppy (I myself always make a point of wearing only a new or freshly pressed white coat) yet there they are, exhausted, slouching almost defiantly in their slept-in hospital uniforms. What are they thinking, I wonder. And I hear my stately voice still hanging in the air. *The lesson of pride.* The lesson of pride, indeed.

And I think, some lessons are so hard to learn. And I see the struggling Ramon striving to teach me still.

The Magic Blue Pill

O h, what if…she had thought way back then
when the birth of the magic blue pill was
being proclaimed across the land, when news-
casters and comedians were going berserk and
leering commentators declared: *Now men had
their pill*! What if it had only come along a year
earlier!

And now as she paced back and forth by
the arrival gate at O'Hare waiting for Ben she
experienced again that flooding of memories
the news had unleashed, exquisite details that
had caused her to click off the chattering heads
and stare at the screen, completely unprepared
for what was happening to her, that same rush
of heat that had marked their first embrace,
moments she thought she had channeled into
gauzy, nostalgic scenes to which she could
return now and then—and then only whenever she wished—for elegiac reminiscences.

How *contingent*—as her husband's colleagues would say—was history.

She had met Ben through Charles, her first husband, at a small, pastoral college in California. Both men had just gained tenure, husband Charles in history by means of a dozen or so papers on copper metallurgy of the fertile crescent; Ben in literature, not through any scholarship but more adventurously, since all he had to show for himself were two collections of short stories and a novel-in-progress. Unexpectedly he was championed by those who had been dismissed as a demoralized coterie of geriatric pre-Postmodern eccentrics. In the ensuing battle Ben became a minor *cause célèbre*, even provoking a student demonstration.

Once the grueling insecurities of conditional employment were over, the two couples became close. Now they could accept the risks of friendship. Claire, Ben's wife, was a soft, bosomy, sweet-tempered former grad student, who occasionally opened a desk drawer and looked in on a thesis that might someday, she said, "eventuate" in a published appraisal of an obscure 19th Century English woman poet. While she herself audited classes in what was once—and might someday be again, she said—her field, French literature. The two faculty wives were gratified to discover they both held the unfashionable view: their careers came second to motherhood. They loved their children! With cheerful resolve they attended to their baby-sitting chores, absorbing the hectic, thought-scattering screeches while sharing lunches in each other's kitchen.

And then husband Charles found out about her and Ben.

It was a love affair that had begun with a startling embrace in Ben's office of all places, had never been consummated in the conventional sense, but had proceeded through so many moments of intimacy and passion that she came to the dreaded realization: in her life ahead she would never, ever feel anything like that for husband Charles. At the time she would not accept such compromises. And now? Could she account for, much less excuse, such foolish, anguished, careless, cruel, ecstatic impulses? She could not.

Remarkably, after the divorce, each of them, she and Charles found someone else to marry within a year or two—although perhaps not all that remarkably: they were both still in their thirties and attractive. She followed her second husband, Martin, taking her daughter (for whom she fought like a tigress) and his daughter by a previous marriage to a deanship in a liberal arts college on the outskirts of Chicago, settling into a new way of life and contentment. As for Ben and his wife, Claire, they wept, took long walks, and stayed together.

It turned out the geriatric eccentrics were prescient. Ben went on to produce one critically acclaimed novel after another, bringing notice and honor to the small college that had nearly discarded him. Meanwhile she, through Martin's continuing ascension, acquired influence in choosing Distinguished Lecturers at her new location, which she exercised now for the first time.

The plane was already more than an hour late. She had paced back and forth past all the gift shops and cafes and bars, read the same newspaper headlines, glanced at the same slick magazine covers and Chicago Bulls T-shirts and sweat shirts, inhaled the cross-cutting pungencies of popcorn and beer, roasted nuts and French fries, fish sticks and hotdogs, all the while dodging the flood of travelers pushing and pulling their luggage. And every time she returned to the gate area, she sighed so fretfully that businessmen, even as they shouted into cell phones, glanced at her curiously.

With each minute's delay she realized there had to be a shifting of plans; there was not only the past but the present to consider. Rush hour traffic would have begun. She could not risk trying to take him to the hotel first. They would have to drive directly to the Student Union where an overflow audience was expected for his reading. Rather than the leisurely re-entry into tender feelings she had been hoping for, they would be dealing with practical urgencies.

At last the door was flung open. She looked for him among the faces twisting this way and that for restrooms and connecting gates, waiting companions, baggage claim and ground transportation. Where was he? Would she even recognize him?

There! Bobbing into view with his peculiar bouncing gait. Backpack over one shoulder. She nearly laughed. Still the portly bear—the dancing bear, she had called him. Rumpled brown hair, sun-bleached though a bit more gray, his beard too more grizzled, burnished cheeks, smiling like someone back from vacation, which now, having lived in the dour mid-west, she recognized as the basic, everyday California smile, a smile most outsiders considered insipid and airy, never imagining its possessor capable of brooding upon the same dark ironies of life as those who lived in harsher climates. And yet, there *was* an undeniable innocence to him. He had boarded the plane in LA, wearing a garish plaid sport jacket, tieless shirt and baggy khaki's, but no overcoat—completely unprepared for the freezing autumn that awaited them outside.

They embraced…Again that first embrace! In his out-of-the way basement office, one that no other self-respecting faculty member would have accepted, one that he made unforgettably his own, filling it with sprawling piles of books and papers, walls of bizarre pictures around the overstuffed couch and chairs, proofs of his amazing energy, how she had become suddenly flushed and wet, how she had used this as proof that yes, this was a man taking risks for.

Although, this time, this embrace, to any observer, was simply a warm greeting between old friends—she was conscious of keeping that pose: the Visiting Author being met at the airport by his Designated Hostess—he secure in his offbeat celebrity, she scrupulously proper-looking, the official representative of the college, who happened to have a long elegant neck under short stylish hair and a handsome black overcoat and flattering chalk-striped suit, appointed to escort him to the campus on the occasion of one of his many public readings.

Even their written communications leading up to the event had stayed true to the moral imperative: no one was to know. They had tried to keep their affair secret. Last time it was she who had failed. This time she would not. By tacit agreement their correspondence had been so exquisitely nuanced, official oversight would have found not even a hint of impropriety. A word here or there in her formal invitation and his honored acceptance could be spotted and the full intent of its subtext decrypted only by the other.

Only when they were safely in her car and on the highway did she, smiling in anticipation, let her hand fall between his thighs. In the past she would have been careful, indeed reluctant to make that bold gesture. Now, she was confident they could call upon the magic blue pill.

It was when she and Ben became lovers that she learned of his...problem. Nowadays it was inscribed in lofty medical Greek: Erectile Dysfunction. Those days it was termed more bluntly: Impotence. The problem, which had been intermittent, he said, when he was younger, seemed to intensify not as a consequence of age—he was not that old, after all—but as he became more immersed in his fictional world. She sympathized, reassured him: had not the great Flaubert chosen celibacy when writing *Madame Bovary*? For me, he said, it's not a choice. It was as though the incubus that ruthlessly commanded the writing and rewriting had seized not only his soul but his whole body, crushing him in its grip. Indeed, she learned to tell when his work was going well because, paradoxically, his marvelous deep voice would become choked into a hoarse whisper. On those days he could barely speak, as though the silent scream that spilled out such eloquent secrets to the page could not be released any other way.

His wife, sweet, bosomy Claire could accept his indisposition, it seemed. But she could not, as she discovered on many tear-filled occasions in his office, in his bed, in her bed, even once in a motel. She needed the fulfillment, the reassurance, of that consummating act, could not live without it. It was the opposite of husband Charles—who performed unfailingly—yet just as bad. Indeed, so fraught had she become, it was she who had let the secret blurt from her one night after too much wine to that unjustly betrayed good man.

They made it to the Student Union barely in time. The audience was restless, overflowing. Students and even townspeople who could not find chairs had arrayed themselves amid piles of parkas and overcoats on the floor at his feet. To her delight he was in excellent form, holding their attention with his best resonant baritone voice—he was between books, enjoying his fame, she could tell—his wry, bushy, expressive face, and repertoire of whimsical, self-effacing gestures, all enhanced, made more profoundly tragicomical, by his strange plaid jacket. Yes, this was the man she had loved, had found worth taking risks for.

He read portions of his latest novel, portions he had chosen carefully to provide a dramatic rise and fall of style and content. When he was finished, there was a palpable silence before he said, "Thank you," and the audience erupted in shouts and applause. The questions were almost all prefaced by expressions of affection and praise. All the while she could see her reflection in the mirror behind him, her long graceful neck craning this way and that as she beamed in sedate approval from her seat in the front row.

The line to collect his autograph on books extended back and forth in two long rows. As she sat waiting for him, watching him at work, she let herself enjoy every inch of his visible flesh, lips that smiled shyly in response to expressions of admiration (she had kissed those lips), eyes that alighted on each face, imparting a glow of pleasure (they had once stirred such a glow from her naked body), ears nearly buried in hair, (how she had loved pressing her face in his hair, finding those ears and running her tongue over their delicate rims). And his soft, expressive hands, the way they moved, the way they caressed each book he signed, each hand they grasped. As she sat there decorously clothed she imagined them gliding under her clothes and over her breasts.

And then at last they were together in her car driving to his hotel, he shivering and laughing and stamping his feet on the floor until the heater warmed him up. In the darkness ornamented by flickering headlights and taillights, they proceeded to explore what had been barely unearthed on the frantic trip from the airport. Yes, he said, Claire was well, had even picked up where she had left off on her thesis and was starting to work on it again, there might indeed be a book out of it, their daughter meanwhile falling passionately in love for the first time—with her horse. Yes, she said, Martin was doing well, happy in his job, an admired administrator— he had already been short-listed for several small college presidencies—a good solid man, much like Charles. You know what they say about second husbands, how much they are like the first, one wonders why people go to all the trouble, she laughed ruefully—and, yes, her daughter too was finding an outlet for adolescent passion in the animal kingdom—no horse, but a dog, cat, numerous rabbits, ducks, she had even requested a goat. Holidays and summers, of course, she and Martin had to attend to the grim business of prisoner exchange, shuttling children back and forth to their ex's.

And you, Ben said finally.

And I, she said with sigh of relief. Am happy to be with you.

He brought her hand to his lips and kissed it. I too, he said. The words, almost classic in simplicity, accompanied by the gesture, seemed to resound far beyond the silence of the car, in a far more enormous space, she thought with a kind of grief that brought tears to her eyes, called time.

She asked if he had thought of her at all, adding quickly to make it easy for him, I know it's good to get over old loves.

Maybe a year ago, he said, as though the words were less uttered than abandoned, it occurred to me that for the first time I was not thinking of you every day.

Again that leaping heat, that restless mix of anxiety and joy. So, he too had continued to love, even as much as she. Except that… what?…had he at last been able to put to an end to it? She told him she was lucky. Or perhaps unlucky. She had more reminders. Because, she said, I read everything you write. Although, to be honest, she admitted, I too thought I had managed to put you away. Some place safely in the past.

And?

And I realized I had not.

They had reached the turnoff to the hotel. As she entered the drive she suddenly realized they had not clarified their options. What now? Should she drive to the bright, arcaded entrance and let everyone see her drop him off, then park and discretely follow after him? Or drive to the parking lot and leave the car there while the two of them casually and boldly strolled in together? It struck her they had never really talked about this precise moment. Yet, did it matter? Whatever they chose to do this precise moment, or indeed any moment from now on, wasn't the objective, the finale obvious? Was this not what she had prepared for, what they had agreed to in their cryptic correspondence, and what they were leading up to, indeed acknowledging, in their conversation? They would go up to his room and make love. They would consummate their affair at last, complete that one longing incompletion. She headed for the parking lot.

Ben spoke first. I'm still the same, he said with a warning quaver.

It doesn't matter, she said brightly, perhaps a bit too impulsively. Now we have the magic blue pill, don't we.

The magic blue pill?

You know what I mean. *Now men have their pill!* She said the words in a mocking kind of glee. But, you see, we women have that pill, too. She reached into the pocket of her suit, felt about in the cool silken recess and drew out the tiny packet that had been waiting there all night. She had enclosed it in Saran Wrap and now held it before them where it shined under the overhead light of the parking lot.

He looked at it, blinking.

Could he be so exasperatingly obtuse at this delicate moment? Don't you see? It's the magic blue pill. You know what I mean. She shook it, emphasizing its importance, like a glowing jewel, an offering, in her hand.

His expression turned to amusement, a good sign, she thought. Finally he got it, and treating it lightly, too. He was not offended. How...? He started to ask.

Shall I tell you? Oh yes. Martin too. All men ultimately have need of the magic blue pill, don't they. And so do we, don't we? Young women take care to carry condoms. But we of a certain age...well...anyway...He'll never know. This time I promise. No one will know.

She waited for him to speak. A moment.

But already in less than a moment she knew: the silence was too long. Less than a moment; yet it was enough.

As she bent her head in mourning Ben took her hand in both of his and kissed it, but only after slowly and firmly closing her fingers over the shiny object.

Driving away from the hotel, she became aware again of the heat, the wetness, but this time it was as though the wetness had come from outside her body, drenching her, as though she had been thrown into a swamp.

With a sob, she opened the window and hurled the shiny package with its magic blue pill out into the rushing darkness, which with a fierce, cold breath devoured it.

Creative Acts

(A Modern Fable)

They both had heard the warnings: They were on the descending slope of their creative powers. He was 29, nearing 30. She 39, almost 40. He was a graduate student in math struggling to complete a thesis for his PhD. She was a securities analyst trainee seeking motherhood.

The warnings were discouraging, of course, so they worked hard to be supportive of each other. He pored over her temperature charts. She endured his insomnia. They saw their creative acts as requiring synchronized efforts.

The days she returned home from her cubicle in San Francisco to their apartment in the Berkeley flats and saw from his shell-shocked face that his latest hope to solve the interlinked four-dimensional sphere problem had been swept away in that day's graduate topology seminar, she would take over. She would drop her briefcase and folders, and, still dressed in her power suit of pinstripe and sheer stockings, strip his clothes off his limp body, start dinner, and return to give him a full body massage and whatever else his weary heart desired.

The nights he found her weeping over the toilet, fouled with yet another gruesome, heartbreaking clot one or two tantalizing weeks after the urine test had been positive, he would take over. He would put his arm around her, lead her back to bed and hold her while she cried, make breakfast, call in sick for her, shop, make the bed, buy her flowers.

They knew the important thing was to never stop trying, to never give up. Had they not both overcome obstacles to get where they are? She in a crowd of six brothers and sisters had migrated from Guatemala to New York, where they continued to migrate from one condemned flat to another—never more than two small dark rooms, including bathroom and sink. Even the pigs and chickens on their little patch of farm back home had more space. She was the first in her family to go to college.

His obstacles were more subtle. He was a corny blonde from Minnesota who lumbered into the Big Apple with his acoustic bass. Looks of disdain, of disbelief greeted this hulking Swede, and he was slow to catch on, but he persisted, hanging around the clubs until the early morning hours when they let him sit in. Then he would smile, crease his eyes and let his thick, velvety fingers do the talking. It turned out he had the goods. And so he made his sunny way into the dark New York jazz world as an occasional sideman.

They had met one night at Sweet Basil. Later they took a CCNY summer school calculus class together. She was determined, she told him, to find a better life by making lots of money in portfolio management. As for him he liked math and was content to wander in and out of whatever courses appealed to him. He hadn't even thought about going for a degree until she made it clear to him he had to get serious about his future. She had no intention of marrying a wandering minstrel.

And even now their creative acts followed the same trajectories. Her goal was specific and palpable, a baby. His goal was so insubstantial it could be imagined by no more than a handful of people in the entire world, a ghostly puff of two spheres that floated in four dimensions, whose intersections were or were not points.

They were determined, however, to be part of each other's efforts.

He followed the chart provided by the fertility clinic as meticulously as she. No need to remind him of the day, the hour, the position, the time required for her to remain on her back after the act to allow the last laggard sperm to find its destined path. He was her dedicated collaborator.

As for her she strained, really strained, to imagine the world of floating spheres he tried to conjure up from his yellow pad. She would get as far as the first infolding and conjunctions, even as far as the transections—he was about to illustrate how the fourth dimension created points out of surfaces—when she became lost. Vainly she stared as his penciled images bulged and twisted. Face bent over the paper, cheeks solidly anchored in her fists, she tried to imagine soap bubbles flailing in the air. She was rooting for him so badly even though she did not know what exactly she was rooting for. But the important thing is *he* knew, and she knew that one day the floating soap bubbles would reveal their secrets to him, she knew they would.

If they both would just keep trying and never give up.

To change his luck he tried changing his patterns. He would take different routes to the office he shared with two other grad students (three desks, one blackboard) in the math department building high up on the Berkeley campus. Sometimes he would stick to the paths, sometimes he would deliberately find ways to make his own path, stomping through bushes and redwood groves, hopping across the rocks in Strawberry creek and in and out and up and down the stairs of interloping buildings. Sometimes he would circle in from the south, sometimes from the north. Sometimes he would ride his mountain bike, sometimes he would walk.

He tried dropping quarters into the outstretched paper cups of panhandlers. He even paused to talk to them, looking for inspiring clues in their deep, elusive philosophies. Once he crouched down to help three fetid, punk-garbed kids with spiked hair and facial studs and safety pins and rings, who were sitting in the gutter bent over a New York Times crossword puzzle.

The idea, of course, was to shake up the wiring in his brain. Like electroshock therapy. He even thought of trying drugs, cigars, skinhead shaves, horror movies, suntan salons, gay bars, topless shows, new sexual positions—although he had to be careful about the last to conserve his volume and potency. In the end, all he dared to do was increase his cappuccino intake, which resulted only in severe intestinal distress and bleeding hemorrhoids. It had no effect on his creativity.

She too had her stratagems. She consulted curanderas, palmists, psychics, mystics, clairvoyants—without telling him, of course. She varied her diet, sneaking into her bag lunches items bought at little shops with beaded curtains and hand-lettered signs—gritty cakes made of buckwheat, millet and mung bean, dried mushrooms and alfalfa, blue-green algae, exotic roots and berries, herbs with names like ginseng, dong quai and fenugreek, vitamins and enzymes, bone meal, goat's milk and rabbit meat—and she too suffered from queasy intestinal rebellions, although she was spared the bleeding hemorrhoids.

She did deep breathing, chanting, imaging, meditation, prayer. She even visited a Catholic church while on a company training session in L.A—without telling him, of course—and kneeled before the garish figure of Jesus and begged him to help her. She carried with her only a dim memory of that stretched-out man—her father had wrenched them from the Church when she was barely three because it had sided with the *patrones.*

This shiny California version seemed less tormented—more like a movie star acting the part—even so she hoped he would be sympathetic. She whispered that it would have to be natural or not at all. They could not afford high-powered technology and frozen embryos. And even though the half-naked man staring in the air seemed preoccupied with his own thoughts, she hoped he would hear her. But period followed period, broken only by the occasional cruel clot.

As they pursued their lonely missions they never forgot about the other. Theirs was a synchronized effort, after all. Weekend afternoons when they finally took time out to relax they weren't really relaxing. Stretched out on the lawn chair in their tiny backyard she never lost her tenacity. She had finished her day's reading assignment involving Dispersion Measurement within a Size-Weighted Composite in preparation for her Chartered Financial Analysts exam. Now behind her sunglasses she surveyed the clouds, constantly on the lookout for shapes that could lead her to understand his search. While he, in shorts and straw hat, put away his reprints on low-dimensional topology and took up medical textbooks devoted to human reproductive functions and dysfunctions. Whatever they could do to help the other they would do. Because, of course, their goals were the same—motherhood and a PhD.

Not that they did not have other occupations in their life. Every working day she awoke before dawn (as her family had done back in Guatemala and still did in New York), put on her power suit and red tie over monogrammed white shirt made of luminous one hundred percent cotton, snapped on her BlackBerry, and joined the sleek, predatory traders swarming into San Francisco where she proved to be, as all her superiors agreed, an animal in the emerging market sector. She was a quick study, mastering Brady Bonds, Eurobonds, foreign debt rating, venture participation, and market capitalization, ignoring jealousies and subtle snubs by the mostly white male Ivy Leaguers manning the banks of computers around her, scaring them away by the sheer intensity of her dedication. Someday soon, her rivals had to concede, she would be handling her own portfolio.

And he kept up his jazz. Local musicians who heard about him, old friends touring from New York—all called him to join them on gigs, so that most weekends and evenings, he kept himself busy doing what he liked best, playing music and imagining math.

Except that the clock continued to tick. Spiteful gods spurned their prayers, their joyous desirings, and taunted them from an impenetrable darkness.

What did they want, these gods? What rites of propitiation were the two of them failing to perform? Time was closing in. University policy allowed him only one more year to complete his thesis and place his footnote in the history of mathematics; else all hopes of an academic life with security of tenure that would give him time for jazz were naught. His life, their life—he would have gambled and lost. And for her, nearing forty, each passing month was like the solemn drumbeat of an approaching funeral cortege.

To keep up their spirits they told each other encouraging stories. His featured the usual legends of long-barren couples who adopted finally and then were inundated with offspring of their own biological conjunctions. Was he trying to suggest they adopt, she asked. No, not really, he said. Just saying we should never stop trying, never give up. Then wondered. Was that all he was saying?

A disconcerting experience. In the worlds he inhabited, psychological self-examination was not a familiar practice.

For her part, she told him a story she remembered from high school chemistry, the only thing she remembered, she said. A scientist named Kekule, after years spent trying to figure out the structure of certain carbon molecules, finally collapsed in exhaustion and had a dream that the carbon molecules formed little dancing rings. When this Kekule awoke he realized that the dream had revealed the solution. The carbon molecules were in the shape of rings. Are you saying I should work harder, he asked. Until I collapse in exhaustion? No. But when you do manage to sleep, she answered, maybe you should check out your dreams. It was a strange notion. All day long he lived in the dream worlds of music and math. He never thought of exploring what went on at night.

These exchanges, of course, had edges. Sometimes they signaled impatience, expressed frustration. They had to be careful not to fight. Among the discouraging things they had heard was that fragile marriages came apart in the pursuit of parenthood. Which also applied to stressed-out graduate students pursuing their PhD. They reminded each other not to over-interpret offhand remarks, not to take personally explosions of temper, to accept with grace a certain waning of romantic and mathematic passion. Love in all its forms suffered from deadlines.

But truth was, the deadlines would not go away. Each new day reminded them, brought new despair. There had to be a way. Babies came. Four-dimensional spheres existed. Nature provided those certainties. They just had to remember to never stop trying, to never give up.

And then the gods struck as only gods can in that part of the world. First was an earthquake (Richter 6.1, epicenter 2.4 miles northeast) that sent pots, pans, dishes and books crashing to the floor. He was alone in the apartment at the time and just managed to clamber down the swaying, groaning stairs and into the street before the building split into huge cracks and tilted to one side. There he became nearly seasick in the spasms of aftershocks as everything around him—trees, buildings, telephone poles—underwent episodic orgies, filling the sky with dust, as from old, battered cushions.

Hours later they managed to reach each other by phone and learn they were both safe. Her office skyscraper in San Francisco had trembled but stood firm. Their old Berkeley apartment though was uninhabitable, would have to be torn down.

Then followed weeks of delicate negotiations with city officials before they got permission to enter the ruin and recover the few clothes and books that had not been looted and pack them into boxes which they carted to another house—a barely refinished garage, actually—up in the hills. They had just finished stacking their boxes around their bed and table when all this, the house, their possessions, everything was consumed in a massive inferno that swept down the Berkeley hills propelled by the Santa Ana winds.

Enough, she said. Guatemala, for all its faults, was never like this. She demanded they get away from crowded cities and overbuilt hillsides. She would find a job at a branch bank. He could pursue his PhD by e-mail. With only their car and the clothes on their backs they made their way further north up to where the Sacramento Valley spread out in rural serenity, and rented a room from a pecan farmer.

A few weeks later, however, a huge flood unleashed by melting Sierra snow glutted the flat farmland and chased them out of the house. Crossing a bridge they were hit broadside by the onrushing water, turned over and over and barely escaped with their lives. Their car was a total loss, even their clothes were useless. They spent sixteen days in Red Cross cast-offs, eating Red Cross rations, along with dozens of other families in a high school gym layered with Red Cross cots.

His nights were spent drifting in and out of insomnia and vivid dreams. As he lay there amid the smells and snores of sleeping strangers he could not get the images of their recent disasters out of his mind—the swaying buildings and trees and telephone poles, the billowing clouds of dust, the swirling fire and smoke and most terrifyingly the roaring, flashing jaws of water that had opened and engulfed their car and sent them turning over and over before disgorging them against a huge fallen tree.

It came to him suddenly that the world was full of such amorphous forces. Against them man's timid straight-line constructions, even his towering skyscrapers, were like puny toothpick toys. He knew this now. The knowledge had become embedded in his soul. He had stared into the very center of the universe and discovered its deep chaos. Who said his form of math was merely theoretical? It was nothing less than the very reality of nature itself.

And then—as though all his brain connections had been torn out and connected anew—the interlocking four-dimensional spheres suddenly sprang to light, herniating out of those amorphous shapes that had been terrorizing his dreams. Power was restored. Now, without cause, without effort, without rhyme or reason, bloated, shimmering bubbles burst to the surface. The solution to the problem he had been seeking simply floated before him. Now it was obvious, now he was sure.

And she, as she lay there on her cot listening to the sounds of strangers, afraid to sleep and face the nightmares that had afflicted her since their ordeals, suddenly realized that for several months—since her supply had been among her possessions looted following the earthquake—she had not required tampons. The thought had crossed her mind before, of course, only to be erased by another disaster. And what an inconvenience it would have been. She tried to remember. How long had she gone without? Four months at least.

She touched her breasts—how strange they felt to her, her nipples unexpectedly full and tender. And then lay her hand on her belly, concentrated her attention and became aware of the brief flutter. Yes, there! Who could have noticed such a delicate thing amid all the violent distractions?

And so, they achieved their desires. She gave birth to a beautiful child with two first names, Ernesto Bjorn (it would be left to him to choose between them). He published his PhD thesis ("A Unique Solution to the Intersecting Four-Dimensional Sphere Problem") to high acclaim from the select handful around the world.

They both went on to distinguished careers—he in math, she in portfolio management—and raised their beautiful child in a beautiful home overlooking the Pacific Ocean. It was, she said, because they had never stopped trying, they never gave up. And he agreed. Indeed, years later she would teach their child and he would teach his students those very lessons: *You must never stop trying, you must never give up.* For that is what mothers and teachers must do.

Yet each had a secret never shared. *Achieved* their desires? Not really. Everything had *happened* to them—that was all. As though at a board meeting of those spiteful gods a decision had been made that once again the world was stale, boring, needed a bit of touching up. The action taken, a jaded compromise wearily arrived at after acrimonious debate, was to accommodate all the competing proposals— earthquakes, fire, floods, whatever—lunchtime, they were getting hungry, these would be their creative acts for the next celestial quarter until they met again.

And naturally in recording the minutes of the contentious meeting and actions agreed upon, unavoidable errors occurred, a few typos. A misplaced comma, an incomplete sentence, a slightly misquoted word, something hardly worth noticing. So that when the decisions were put into effect minor unintended externalities occurred. Freeways collapsed crushing scores of cars meanwhile opening a thrilling vista to the Ferry Building, a cherished landmark. Flames devoured all but one house on a hillside, a modest bungalow amid surrounding mansions, which, stripped clear of trees, soared in value with its multi-million-dollar panoramic view. Swirls of water from the raging flood slapped aside a whole street of houses and left a single clothesline of underwear fluttering brightly in the air.

Trivial, unavoidable side effects. A birth here, a discovery there. Beneath notice by the gods.

And everything, everything to mortals.

Have A Beautiful Day

Hot Air Balloons

O ld Uncle Sam—I can still hear my father's ironic mockery every time I say his name—Uncle Sam likes when I set him where he can watch the hot air balloons. A company called Have a Beautiful Day Hot Air Balloons launches tourists and conventioneers from the beach. As the balloons catch the evening breeze and rise over the park you can hear the roar of the torch and see the faces of the people in the bannered gondolas. Have a Beautiful Day the baskets cheerfully command. Mr. Do from the nursing home and I sit on a bench alongside the wheelchair. The kids in the park—mostly Vietnamese like Mr. Do—will wave to the people overhead and if they wave back the kids shriek and laugh and fall all over each other. The ocean is a dull pewter, as though the low sunlight has skimmed off its sheen, the balloons radiant in the last broadside. Some Sundays as many as a dozen or so, striped and spiral-colored, fill the sky. We follow them as they float over the rumbling interstate and vast marsh of clay tile roofs toward the mountains, gradually shrinking like tiny drops of wine sliding down into the burgundy haze.

You think he's comfortable, I always ask.

Oh, yes, Mr. Do always answers.

Somehow he manages to get my uncle into a grey suit and polished loafers, a handkerchief fluffed in his breast pocket. Under his baseball cap a twist of mouth, a smile actually.

Happy? Really happy?

Oh, yes. Very happy.

I watch as Mr. Do pulls out Uncle Sam's handkerchief and wipes his face. Like a bird brushing about a piece of garden statuary.

I remember I am—what?—four, perhaps five years old, looking up at this strange man swabbing his bald head, embracing a brown paper bag. Jacket and pants droop in mismatched patterns of grey. Even that child could recognize they come from different suits. The man gives his mouth a strange twist: Not something you expect to find on your doorstep, am I.

This is your Uncle Sam, my father says, without looking at either of us.

That night at dinner this Uncle Sam asks me: So what do you want to be when you grow up, young man, digging the words out of his throat the way my father does. It's not the slurring effortless speech I hear from everyone else—like warm sand running through your fingers—and I realize for the first time that my father too comes from another place.

A doctor, I say.

The man looks at my father. You see. It runs in the family.

My father's gruff answer surprises me. So what does that make me—the family idiot?

Later I hear them downstairs. Everyone has troubles, my father rages. Look what happened to *him*—he had to drop his used car business and scramble to find work at Convair. Otherwise it was the army. Even though he had a kid. Just when business was picking up. Whole trainloads of families arriving every day to be near their men in uniform. Willing to pay *anything*. And now the damn blackout in case of Japanese invaders. What did H.V. Kaltenborn call them? Yellow Peril! *Orientals!* Not even human!

I crouch by the window, terrified that I might see monstrous Oriental submarines with slanted eyes and thick glasses rising from the moon-glittering water. Then I creep back to my bed and while they continue quarreling lie there in the dark listening to the radio, hearing my father's taunts through the music.

So, what did you expect from your little brother, Uncle Sam? What do you expect from the family idiot?

He doesn't even go to Hebrew school.

Here nobody speaks Hebrew.

When he grows up, what will he be?

Smarter than you, Uncle Sam. Bet on it!

Until he could pass an exam and practice medicine again Uncle Sam went to work selling cars, filling in during my father's shift at Convair. I remember him bobbing around the lot behind the darting strides of my father, trying to pick up sales techniques—the same ones my father later taught me before I took over the dealership. Such as letting a customer drive a car home for a few days before paying for it. (Watch the eyes. Some people you do them a favor, they're hooked.)

A disaster.

The Ford coupe with leatherette covers, Uncle Sam! The Plymouth with only three thou on it. Where'd they go?

People cheat. What can I do?

The eyes, I said, watch their *eyes*.

But Uncle Sam found no answers in the eyes.

Night after night contempt and exasperation boil up in my father's voice, usually ending with his providing a long list—brothers and sisters, aunts, uncles, cousins, all of them professors, doctors, *bigshots* as fancy and

distinguished as Uncle Sam pretended to be—
all named with a vengeance. Why didn't he go
to *them* for help?

Gently, always gently, Uncle Sam reminds
him they all are gone.

So? So? You should have left when the family idiot did! And a door would slam.

And I would hear Uncle Sam acknowledge
in the silence that yes, his little brother had
outsmarted them all.

The night before Uncle Sam moves out, the
mild-mannered man finally lets his temper fly.
I hold my breath at what I hear. *Shit for brains!*
Did he think he hadn't *tried* to get out? Their
old father stubborn...mother hopeless...the
children...*He at least remembered his responsibili-
ties!* They got as far as Paris, where the police—
the *police, no less!*—grabbed their papers and
ordered them into a huge stadium that was
used for bicycle races. Separated into long
lines and made to stand for hours. Thousands
of people. Just before she was taken away
Moira his daughter begs him, Why must I do
this? Haven't I been a good girl?

I don't remember the answer Uncle Sam
gave to his daughter. I was busy picturing
the scene—shaping it from the lights cast on
the ceiling by my radio. A huge stadium just
for bicycle races! I could imagine what that
was like. My father had started taking me to

high school football games. People shouting, waving flags, singing, while bands played and cheerleaders jumped and did cartwheels and pyramids, my father never failing to point out to me his advertisement in the program they gave out. It had a picture of a soldier and sailor carrying American flags.

By the time I returned to Uncle Sam's story he was in the back of a truck with other men. The truck broke down and they had to get out and hurry to the train. Along the way people jeering.

My father protests. He doesn't want to hear these things.

You *will* hear these things, Uncle Sam shouts. He pauses for breath. We get to the station. A huge crowd now. Each sentence is like a massive door he has to push open. We're standing around. Waiting. And all of a sudden. I take one little step. To the side. Like this. That's all, just like this—his voice made an odd squeak—and I start jeering, too. And that's how I got left behind. I became one of them. One of those people.

Even from my bed I could tell what his face looked like, his strange twist of a smile.

You'll see. Now you'll be rich, was all my father said. Here all the doctors are rich.

And that was the last I saw of Uncle Sam until the synagogue from L.A. called me. Their computer system had sounded the alert. He was delinquent on his pledge. I was listed on his file card. Did I know anything about it? A doctor, too. Usually they're so reliable.

Mr. Do gets up and adjusts Uncle Sam's baseball cap, which keeps sliding to the side. He leans over to hoist him up in the wheelchair. The two men embrace, look briefly at each other—a smile—then Mr. Do sits back down. We continue to gaze at the balloons and at the slowly shifting sunset hues on the mountains beyond them.

I realize I am touched by the way Mr. Do hugged my uncle.

You miss your home, I ask. It is the first time I venture a personal question.

Mr. Do shrugs.

The lightness of the gesture takes me by surprise, offends me. Is that it? The Vietnam war—a *shrug!* And my response surprises me, too. It is almost a lunge, a physical bursting out of long-buried resentment. Has he already forgotten, I hear myself scolding him. The victims. Not only his Vietnamese people and our American soldiers, the dead and maimed. Others he probably did not even know about. Those of us who fought against the war back home. Crippled by rashly made choices. Prison. Canada. Still stuck in a charred bitterness that cannot be scoured. So much hate in this country now, unforgotten, unforgiven, and I hear myself go on at length about how

I had marched and demonstrated, how I had screwed up my chance of medical school and fought with my father and broke with my woman, and yes, spent a night in jail.

Mr. Do does not seem exactly swept away by my lament. And in fact I am annoyed at myself for being so provoked by his shrug. His smile remains blandly unmoved, a geisha smile, hands folded in his lap.

So, I ask, impatiently, but determined to be tolerant: What did you do in Vietnam? He had been the enemy after all, the side I had been demonstrating against. I try to engage his eyes.

Doctor.

Doctor. No kidding. I am surprised, actually. And let my voice rise to signify that I'm impressed. No kidding. I nod in the direction of Uncle Sam. So was he, you know.

Mr. Do nods. He knows. The geisha eyes, I realize, never look at me directly.

You knew that?

Oh, yes.

You hoping to practice again someday?

Oh, yes. Mr. Do nods.

You'll have to take some kind of test.

Yes. Take test. Though he can barely speak English he makes it seem so easy. Yet I think what magic these little people possess, the tricks they can do. Everywhere you look there are their children, barely settled in and already winning spelling bees and scholarships, filling newspapers with headlines of their honors and awards.

That's what he had to do.

Mr. Do smiles blandly, nods.

I describe how while waiting to take the test for a medical license Old Uncle Sam tried selling cars. I laugh at the memory. Then become embarrassed by the sound of my voice, the echo of my father's contempt for the doctor's ineptitude. Is Mr. Do offended? His eyes are resting peacefully on the balloons, which are miles away now, no more than festive ornaments hanging in the sky.

How did you manage to get out?

Silence.

Then I heard the word.

Boat.

He accompanied it with the briefest twist of a smile.

So, he was one of the famous boat people. Not so long ago—when was it?—they too had their fifteen minutes, their headlines and feature stories, their television specials. Overloaded hulks. Thai pirates. Rapings, lootings, murder. I look at him. Could this delicate creature have survived anything as terrible as that?

What was it like? I said, meaning of course, what was it really like.

Mr. Do smiled. Boat sank.

How then...?

He shrugged. Lucky. Again that smile.

It helps to be lucky, doesn't it.

He nodded.

Some people weren't so lucky, I suppose.

He nodded.

Who? People you knew?

Again a silence. Then the words.

Wife. Children.

It was my turn to be silent. I simply could not speak. As though my mouth were filled with shattered glass. Meanwhile, around me, the world carried on as usual. The balloons now dotted the sky in colorful musical notation, like a jaunty Sousa march. And Uncle Sam continued to smile at the children cheerfully and indignantly squirting water at each other from the fountain.

He lost his family too, I said finally, trying to make up for my clumsiness.

I know.

What? What do you know, I demanded.

The answer scratched against my face. And for a man who must never in his life have heard a remotely similar concatenation of sounds, he pronounced it perfectly.

Auschwitz.

And just then I heard the spurting noise, turbulent and urgent. Right over our heads. Another balloon. Massively alone and seemingly crippled. Apparently it had gotten off late and was in trouble, its torch sputtering on and off.

When the children on the ground caught
sight of the struggling beast they went wild
with laughter. They had never seen anything
so hilarious. In the gondola were four or five
children, waving uncertainly. You could tell by
the way they clung to the wicker sides they were
waving to cover their fear. Have a Beautiful
Day said the flapping red white and blue ban-
ner. Again and again the torch snorted and the
huge shape undulated protestingly, like some
thick liquid trying to dissolve.

Uncle Sam's wheelchair creaked and
I became aware that he was grunting and
twisting.

Mr. Do, I said.

The dainty geisha man leaned over, lis-
tened, then smiled and nodded and gave him
a gentle pat.

What? What's he saying?

Still smiling Mr. Do looked up, shrugged.

He say: Get out.

Now the children were cheering. The struggling balloon apparently was trying to make
its way to the Kmart parking lot just across
the freeway. With each desperate gasp it sank
lower and lower, skimming over the speeding
cars, it's torch snorting convulsively. It managed to stay aloft just long enough to reach the
edge of the tarmac where it squatted with dod-
dering relief, the neon-bright fabric collapsing
and enveloping the basket in one last display,

like a peacock spreading its tail. After a few moments we could see the children beating their way out from under it, flinging their arms and stomping triumphantly. They ran this way and that. I almost imagined I could hear their high-pitched voices, although at that distance and with so many other sounds—the cars, the ocean, the jeers of the children around me—I doubt it. And I caught something else, although I couldn't be sure of that either, again that smile—it passed between the two men.

What? I said to Mr. Do. But he didn't answer. Instead he was staring, both of them were staring, smiling, not at the balloon in the parking lot, but off into the distance at the other balloons, now small and insubstantial as bubbles, descending and one by one disappearing into the wine-dark haze.

About the Author

L.J. Schneiderman is an emeritus professor at the University of California San Diego School of Medicine, where he founded the Family Medicine residency program and was also the founding co-chair of the UCSD Medical Center Ethics Committee.

A recipient of the Pellegrino Medal in medical ethics, Schneiderman has published many medical and scientific works, as well as the novel *Sea Nymphs by the Hour* and short stories. He has been recognized for both his fiction and plays with the Drama-Logue Award, Beverly Hills Theater Guild Award, Pushcart Award nomination, and more.

Schneiderman lives in Del Mar, California.

Made in the USA
San Bernardino, CA
19 November 2014